The beginning and the end
After sitting in the drab, frosty waiting forever, an unfamiliar voice broke the sil see you now,' I followed the plump recepɫɩѻɳɩѕɫ ѡɩɫɦ until we reached Dr. Daw's room, wondering what had become of her old receptionist, dreamy Daniel. The only reason I used to turn up half an hour early to my sessions was so that Daniel and I would have an excuse to talk for a while, and when I say talk I mean passionately kiss in the storage cupboard for 20 minutes like a couple of naughty school children not wanting to get caught. I quickly tapped out a text to Mr. Dreamy asking where he'd moved onto before entering the oh-so familiar office of my counsellor Dr. Daw. The room itself was simple; mint green and light with potted plants placed perfectly along the bottom of the floor to ceiling window, I suppose it was decorated in a way that would make people feel calm. I slumped down on the cream leather sofa, opposite Dr. Daw sat royally in her arm chair. She was a skinny lady with bright blonde hair twisted onto the top of her head and held there with a jewelled clip. I had observed over the years of seeing her that not a strand of hair on her perfect little head was ever out of place, it was kind of irritating.

'Hi, again,' I smiled half-heartedly.

'Brooke, this is the longest you have gone without seeing me, it must have been over a year since our last session?' she asked. She spoke very quietly, but confidently as always. 'What brings you back?'

'It's pretty fucked up,' I stated, 'I wouldn't know where to start,'

She chuckled at my brutal honesty, 'well we can only start at the beginning…'

I breathed in, still unsure whether I wanted to delve into the deepest darkest parts of my life, to tell her the whole painful, horrendous truth, but I was sitting in that room again and there was no turning back now, I had to tell someone, and this time I couldn't hold anything back.

December

'Why haven't they been arrested?' I wondered out loud as I observed the woman across the street serving another happy customer a bag of drugs as her little boy watched from the cracked window at the front of their house, 'she should have that kid taken away from her.'

'Oh here we go,' Jamie rolled her eyes at me, 'here comes police officer Brooke, the Brooke that is *so* annoying,' she complained as she glissaded a large brush through her lengthy hair. 'Brooke!' Jamie shrieked at me as I continued to stare past her.

I jumped out of my oblivious state and turned to her, 'what?'

'They're none of your business. *Me* on the other hand, your best friend of *17 years* should have your full attention at all times, yes?' she moaned, shaking my shoulders franticly, 'and anyway, isn't the whole point of you working in the police now that you can just go over there and go all Miami Vice on her arse?'

I laughed, 'Jamie, I'm just an apprentice for one, and I'm training in the NCA department, I'm not on the streets, I have reported them so many times though…'

I stopped talking as I noticed Jamie's blank expression, it wasn't that she didn't support me, but Jamie could never understand why I didn't take the easy route and work in my mum's beauty business like she had. Yes, the money was good, and I knew everything like the back of my hand as my mum had trained me up in all areas. I could give you an amazing spray tan, a big bouncy blow dry, lashes to die for and be finished by 5pm every night. But there was one slight problem, I disliked my mum immensely.

Jamie and I had grown up together as our families were very close. My mum had met Jamie's dad, Mike before any of us were born, they had a brief relationship after meeting at the local *Sainsbury's* one night where their trolleys had collided. Mike and my dad had been best of friends ever since secondary school. Mum would bring up the story of how she met my dad at any given opportunity-equally as cheesy and sickening each time she blurted it out.

'We met at a pub one night where Mike and I were having a quick dinner before heading back to our own home, not planning to stay the night together; we were going through a rough patch.' She would always start-emphasising the 'rough patch' so she didn't look like a tart who jumped from one guy to his best friend, which was exactly what had really happened.

'Jerry (my dad) strolled in through the door dressed in skinny jeans, a white shirt with the sleeves rolled up and a smile that would make any girls heart flutter. Mike noticed him and introduced us; he had me from the first cheeky wink after that.'

She would gush, at this point she usually planted a sloppy, inappropriate kiss on my dad's lips as everyone 'awwed' at the happy couple.

'Mike could see that me and Jerry had instantly hit it off and he pulled me over to a quiet corner to talk, saying that he knew we were better as friends and that I could go for Jerry- he thought he would like me. I then dragged Mike to the bar and tried setting him up instantly with a gorgeous girl; he couldn't find any one of taste so he insisted that he left us to it. Jerry and I sat at the bar talking and having one too many drinks until the pub closed; I felt like I had known him for years after that night-so romantic, it was like fate brought us together I always say.'

I usually left at this point making up a silly excuse like I needed to use the toilet or I thought I had left my T.V switched on in my room, but I would always be back down to the crowded room in time to catch the end of the story.

'Mike met Lisa (Jamie's mum) at the library, he was scanning for a gardening book, and funnily enough so was Lisa. They both reached for the same book and *bam!* Sparks flew. We all became very close friends after that, and have been ever since.' She would end the story by raising a glass to 'love, happiness and friendship' before she would be flooded with personal questions and admirable looks, everyone wishing they had the 'perfect life of Claire Hamilton.'

'I'm so excited for tonight! Everyone's going,' Jamie quickly changed the subject. She pouted her rouged lips into the mirror.

'By everyone you mean Luke, right?' I answered half-heartedly, still keeping one eye firmly on the child in the window opposite.

'Luke, who's Luke?' she grinned. She was probably one of the prettiest people I had ever met. Her perfectly straight teeth seemed to glisten against the lights of her Hollywood mirror.

'Well obviously something is going to happen, I mean look at you.' I complimented, sighing as the child's mother yanked the curtains across the window. I ran some lip gloss across my cracked lips in an attempt to look even half as good as my best friend did without even trying.

She laughed as she flicked her long hair over her shoulders and pulled up her tight top, but still her massive cleavage was on show, 'no, nothing will happen with Luke, that was boring me.'

As we wedged our way through avid crowds of teenagers I began to question why I had agreed to join Jamie that night. This was not the right place for a girl with crippling anxiety to be spending her time. I could feel my chest becoming tighter and my vision was turning blurry-those two were always the first signs of a panic attack. *Not now please body.* I begged.

'Oh my god, it's so good here isn't it?' she grinned, holding my arm and leading me towards a tall stand at the far end of the Christmas fair.

'Yes,' I reluctantly agreed; trying to sound at least a tiny bit enthusiastic in an attempt not to hurt her feelings, 'where the hell are you taking me now?' I wondered.

As we drew closer to the stand I noticed that there were not as many people over this end of the capacious circus tent I had been dragged through for the past 3 hours. My chest felt a bit loser, I inhaled and exhaled a few times to bring my heart beat down, just like my counsellor Dr. Daw had told me to do many times.

'It's a Clairvoyant!' she replied excitedly, fastening her pace as she noticed a big group of Goth like 20 something's join the small queue to the stand.

I peered around a tall girl dressed head to toe in black to see the Clairvoyant herself. She was typical of what you would expect; dressed in a long gypsy style outfit with a scarf wrapped around her long, braided hair. I hissed in Jamie's ear, 'why are you making me do this?'

She turned to me and frowned, 'for god sake, can't you live a little? You're becoming your mother you know that?' I gave her a dirty look, but stayed in the line as I did not want to become my mother in any way, shape or form.

When it came to be Jamie's turn, she pushed me in front instead, 'you can go first because I'm so nice,' she grinned. I scowled at her as I walked towards the woman.
'Hello, there,' she smiled at me as I placed myself on the wooden chair in front of her. There was a small table positioned between us, she nonchalantly laid her hand onto it- her long, red fingernails pointed towards me as she did so.

'Hi,' I greeted her politely, 'nice to meet you.'

'You're a lovely girl aren't you, not at all like your mother,' she said as she starred straight into my eyes. She made me feel quite uncomfortable; I fidgeted nervously as I felt her eyes bore into mine. She *must have overheard the conversation Jamie and I had about my mum,* I thought to myself, 'now, give me your hand,' she ordered. I could hear Jamie's high pitched giggle from behind me.

I held my hand out as instructed, but instead of holding it she just stared. After what seemed like an age of silence she whispered, 'you're nervous, why's that my love?'

'I'm not nervous,' I lied. The hand that she had sprucely laid upon the table quickly flew up, making me jerk in my seat. She seized hold of my hand and yanked it forcefully so that it was closer to her. She closed her eyes and I turned around to Jamie; at least she was amused.

'Turn back!' the woman shouted. I did as she said and watched her as she narrowed her forehead in concentration. Her hand began to shake and then she expeditiously let go. Her face turned into a picture of panic, 'well, there is nothing I can do for you,' she said sternly.

'What do you mean?' I laughed, but she dismissed me and signalled for Jamie to take a seat. I grabbed Jamie and pulled her out of the queue, 'we are *not* wasting any more time with that psycho!' I insisted before hurrying her away.
'What the hell did she mean by that?' Jamie laughed as we sat down at a table after spending a fortune on the dessert stand.

'Don't ask me,' I answered as I stuffed in a mouthful of sugary doughnut, jam oozing down my chin. I studied her face, 'you don't really believe any of that crap she just said, do you?' I asked as I wiped my chin with my sleeve.

Jamie looked at me in disgust before replying, 'You hear loads of stories about them being right, don't you?' Her gaze followed a boy who was sliding past the table with a tray of food in his hands- she raised her eyebrows suggestively at me. I turned to look at the boy as he sat down on the table behind us, he looked up and I swiftly pivoted back around in my seat. Jamie however, smiled and waved at him flirtatiously before mouthing to me, 'I told you it would be a good night,'

I looked at her vigorously, 'they will say any crap to make money, don't believe it.' I carried on eating whilst I inspected the crowd. A young boy and girl bolted past us as they headed towards a small ghost train. An elderly woman took a leisurely stroll as she pulled apart her candy floss, humming to herself. I noticed a familiar figure leaning against one of the many poles that were holding the tent up, 'Harriet!' I shouted across the crowds; she didn't answer.

Harriet was one of the few trainees, including me, that were still undertaking their apprenticeships to get a job at the National Crime Agency. We were only 4 months in to our 2 year course, but had become quite close during this time. We had a lot in common and a lot to talk about as we were both gripped constantly by the ever growing rate of organised crime that we witnessed every day. We would spend hours after work debating what we could do to 'make the world a better place' over a bottle of wine or two. I guess we were both dreamers, but I liked that about us.

I was about to walk over to say hello when a boy approached her, Harriet apprehensively looked around while he spoke, they looked as though they were in deep conversation. He was a lanky, dishevelled looking boy; he couldn't have been much older than her.

I observed as the conversation became more and more intense. He grabbed her arm and pulled her closer to his unsanitary looking body. I ascended from my seat, 'can we and talk to Harriet for a minute?' I asked in a way that was more of an instruction than a question.

'B, me and that boy were having major eye chemistry, this Harriet girl better be important,' she whined as I pulled her along behind me.

I ignored her as I dodged between hordes of people. As we grew closer I could faintly hear the boy's sullen voice. I turned to Jamie and placed my finger over my mouth as I guided her a few yards behind Harriet and the boy. I still couldn't hear their conversation over the noise of the fair.

'Is that her boyfriend?' Jamie whispered disapprovingly into my ear.

I shook my head, 'I don't know who he is, maybe we should just go over to her,' the boy looked as though he was becoming angry with her.

I lugged Jamie along after me, 'Hi Harriet,' I smiled. She jumped as she heard me and then gave me a faint hearted smile.

The boy stared at Jamie and I before giving us a threatening look, 'nice to meet you,' I said as I held out my hand for him to shake.
He stared at it rudely and then spat on the floor, 'could you not see we're 'avin a conversation?' he asked us, his voice was deep and profound. He glanced over to Harriet with a worried look in his bloodshot, jaded eyes.

'Don't be rude mate.' Jamie stepped forwards, 'she's only being polite. It's not really that nice to meet you,'

He strolled forwards cockily until he towered over Jamie, 'know your place, babe.'

I watched Jamie cautiously as she stepped closer to him and looked up; she didn't look scared at all, 'don't call me babe,'

He grabbed her arm and Harriet and I both jumped towards her, 'leave her alone, Matt!' Harriet piped up, 'it's not her you have the problem with!'

Jamie and I looked at each other in a state of confusion as he dropped Jamie's arm and shot Harriet an almost apologetic look. Harriet was such a beautiful girl and he was, well the complete opposite. I wondered what she was doing with him, I knew her too well to believe that she wanted a relationship with someone like that.

'Just let me talk to them for five minutes, yeah?' she asked softly as she stroked his arm. She seemed to oddly have some sort of hold over him, he nodded and strolled away, kicking a Coke can across the grass as he did so. Harriet relaxed immediately and stepped towards us shyly, rubbing her hand against her forearm.

'What are you doing with him?' I questioned her.

'Straight to the point as always,' she chuckled timidly, wincing as she did so.

'What's wrong?' I held my hand out to hug her, but she flinched and stepped backwards.

'Nothing, I'm fine. I'm sorry about Matt. He can be…' she paused to think of the correct word to describe her boyfriend, '…intense. He's just got a lot going on, we both have. He is nice really. You know I wouldn't be with him otherwise.'

I nodded, she was usually such a good judge of character that I would never doubt her choice in anything-but there seemed to be more to the story.

'Didn't seem it,' Jamie muttered under her breath.

Harriet glanced at her, 'well you don't know him. We're in love.'
'Love? You're in love with *that*?' Jamie sniggered. I looked over to him, blowing cigarette smoke out of his nostrils and pacing restlessly.

'Yes, do you have a problem with that?' Harriet seemed as though she was earnestly protecting him, like she actually did really care about him.

'Jamie, shut up,' I snapped at her, 'as long as you're okay nothing else matters,' I reassured Harriet. 'I don't think we've been doing the same shifts for ages have we? I haven't seen you for a couple of weeks,' I carried on the conversation, not wanting to leave her so soon.

'I-I haven't been at work actually, I've not been well,' she answered nervously, 'I'm okay now though, I'll be back Monday,' she quickly added before I could ask her what was wrong. I looked over to Jamie and raised my eyebrows, expecting her to apologize, but instead she just childishly shrugged.

'See you around, Harriet,' Jamie muttered before strutting back over to where we had been sitting flicking her hair over her shoulders and pulling out a cigarette from her *Chanel* handbag.

'Don't you want to go after her?' Harriet asked as she led me back to the pole she was standing at before we had interrupted. I noticed that she had lost a lot of weight since I had last seen her.

'No, she's fine,' I smirked as I glanced over and saw that canteen boy had already sat down next to her, 'apart from being ill, how have you been? I questioned, turning back to face her.
'I've been fine, busy,' she answered, tucking a lose strand of hair from her pony tail behind her pierced ears, 'did you hear much about the raid they done on that house the other day?' she frowned as her eyes jolted towards where Matt was pacing.

'Oh god, yeah, they found 4 rooms filled with girls, I think there was like 16 of them. Some of them didn't make it, but they still haven't found whose house it was.' I informed her, remembering the report I had to write up on my previous shift.

'They've been working that case for so long. I hope they find the people behind it all soon,' she sighed.

It was true; the department we were training in had been attempting and failing to find the people behind the biggest human trafficking organisation they have experienced in years. Countless anonymous tips and houses being raided later and it seemed they were none the wiser.

'You look tired,' I frowned as I noticed the big, black bags under her eyes, 'are you sure you're okay?' I clutched the arm that she had been holding the whole time we had been speaking, she grimaced in pain, 'what happened?' I pulled up her sleeve before she could stop me, revealing several dark purple bruises scattered up her arm.

'It's not what it looks like,' she insisted.

'I think it's exactly what it looks like, Harriet, he can't do this to you!' I whispered so no one around us would hear.

'I didn't think you were judgmental, Brooke. He is stressed out; you don't know the half of it,' she rambled.
'We both know that there's no excuse for what he is doing to you,' I stated bluntly.

'It's not as bad as it sounds, trust me! We'll meet up for a drink soon,' she said hastily before hugging me and darting over to Matt.

'Harriet?' I called after her. But she didn't hear me, I watched as he hugged her and said something in her ear; he looked down at her dotingly as he guided her away from the fair.

Frustrated, I strolled back over to Jamie and sat down opposite her and what would probably be her new flavour of the month. He was very tall and muscular with dark hair and baby blue eyes. I grinned at Jamie and she nodded her head in reply- she and I had always had the ability to communicate telepathically, especially when it came to boys.

'Is she okay?' Jamie asked me, 'that was intense.'

'Yeah, she'll be fine,' I smiled, not believing my answer at all.

It was Christmas Eve and I had 2 hours left of work before I could have a whole week off. That was one of the perks of being an apprentice, nobody sees you as relevant enough to stay working over Christmas so to get us all out of the way we'd been given paid holiday. Obviously this was just a ploy to ensure we stayed working there once our training was complete as the department was very understaffed. I was beginning to understand why, as I sat in the bleak, somber briefing room and listened to the latest heart-wrenching discovery of yet another house full of depleted and defiled women who had been harboured there to then be sold onto disgusting men for unimaginable reasons. The constant photographs, recordings and statements that I had to listen to day in day out was enough to make me want a career change, but the fact that we were finding these women before they were exploited was enough reason as any to carry on soldiering through the job each day.

'We received another anonymous tip,' my head of department, the big boss, Mr. Daniels was addressing everyone in the room whilst standing in front of a board filled with possible suspects, photographs and post it notes of questions, 'which led us to this house,' he pointed to the picture of the crumbling house in which the women were being hidden in. 'This address is registered to a Mr. Andrew Spence, 45 years of age,' he pinned the picture of Andrew next to the house on the board, 'this is who we put all of our focus on now, we need to find him and bring him in for questioning as soon as possible. Before any more innocent people have to die or suffer.'

I shivered as I examined the photo he had pinned up. Andrew Spence had a face that looked much senior to that of a 45 year old. His dark brown eyes added a hellish look to his withered face which was framed with what appeared to be a very greasy, matted head of jet black hair.

Mr. Daniels paused for effect as everybody in the room hung onto his every word, writing notes as he spoke and nodding in agreement.

'This department has raided 35 houses this year, 35.' He paused again, making sure he stared at each and every one of us in the eye. 'In those 35 houses we found over 500 women and children. 276 of those were dead on the scene or died later in hospital. This is too many, we must act faster or the figure is going to reach it's thousands. And this is just in our area, in London alone. Modern slavery is becoming an even bigger issue than in previous years. Millions of people around the world are being subjected to this wrongful exploitation and if our little team here can contribute to stopping one major organised crime group then we can sleep well knowing that we are helping in some way, yes?' Everyone nodded in unison. 'So Andrew Spence, we find him and we find out who else is involved. Trainees, I know you're off for Christmas now, but whilst you're at home filling your bellies with mince pies and pigs in blankets please spare a thought for all those millions of people who are spending their Christmas being sold, exploited, used for organs, raped, need I go on?'

Well this got a bit unnecessarily depressing. I thought to myself as I looked around the room at my fellow apprentices, squirming uncomfortably in their chairs as the officers looked at them with a hint of judgment on their faces, or was it jealousy because we could go home for Christmas and they couldn't. Either way, I'd had enough of this deep and dismal lecture. Yes, I understood the severity of the situation, but I also didn't want to be made guilty for enjoying a pig in a blanket or 4.

'Anyway,' Mr. Daniels continued, 'have a lovely Christmas trainees, and the rest of you I will see you here tomorrow bright and early.'

The room buzzed with murmurs of pointless chatter, people saying 'have a lovely Christmas' and 'I'll see you in the morning' as they collected their things and made their way out of the door. I didn't speak to anyone as I hurried out of the building without a second look. I jumped in my car and made my way to my Auntie and Uncle's home where I had spent every Christmas since I could remember.

'Merry fucking Christmas' I said to myself as I breathed a huge sigh of relief.

25th *of December*

As the only conscious soul in the otherwise sleeping house I made a prodigious effort to keep it that way as I crept across the lustrous floorboards which bounded the upper story of my aunt and uncle's home. As I snaked down the grand staircase I glanced at the many family photos held proudly by the walls. My thoughts departed back to a time when I would slide down the steel arms of the staircase to be caught by my doting father at the bottom. As I reached the large kitchen I smiled as I peered out of the frosty window. Snowflakes glided peacefully downwards from the early morning sky, settling on the beautiful garden that lay miles ahead of me. I trembled as my bare feet touched the tiled floor, sending a chill up my visible spine.
'What are you doing up so early, darling?' my auntie gently whispered from behind me.

I tensed as I hadn't heard her enter the room, 'I'm sorry, did I wake you up?' I asked as I watched her glide into the kitchen; she did not make a noise as if she were an angel floating inches above the ground.

Merry Christmas,' she beamed as she kissed me on the cheek- ignoring my question. The warmth that travelled off of her made my goose bumps disappear.

'You too, Veronica,' I replied as I wrapped my arms around her petite neck.
Auntie Veronica-my mother's older sister by 10 years-and I had always been very close, she would repeatedly tell me that from the minute I entered the world she knew we would be the 'best of friends.'
Auntie Ron and Uncle Jeremy had taken me in when I was 7 years old after my parents couldn't handle my constant breakdowns with their, and I quote, 'busy work schedules.'

Veronica had lived through the worst times with me. The debilitating sleep paralysis and night terrors, the constant being sent home from school after being sick and not being able to breathe being just a few. She was the person who pestered the doctors for months to help me after they insisted it was a stomach bug, or something in my diet that was causing the constant illness. All the while my mother had to escape to holistic retreats and extensive therapy to help cope with her, and yes here's another quote from the witch herself, 'out of control child.'

For this reason, along with many others, I had always had a much better relationship with Auntie Veronica than I did my own mother.

The patter of tiny footsteps echoed down the stairs before my excitable twin siblings Riley and Ruby burst through the door, running straight over to the huge Christmas tree and gasping at the tower of presents piled underneath. Their angelic emerald green eyes-filled with wonder and magic- twinkled against the beautiful lights wrapped neatly around the tree,

'Merry Christmas sweeties,' I whispered, planting a kiss on their tiny foreheads.

'Aha!' Veronica resounded from the other side of her vast front room. Her voice echoed as she jumped up from the chair she was perched on, 'I know what it is!'
Everyone's bewildered expressions turned to face her, the lights from the towering tree reflected against her hideous chandelier earrings, blinding us all in the process.

'What? How in the world could you know what *that* is?' My uncle exclaimed from the long dining table behind her between mouthfuls of homemade chocolate cake. He squinted across the room at my mum-obviously misplacing his glasses again-she was standing in the centre of the room fluctuating her arms around in a drunken attempt to play charades.

'What am I acting out then, Ron?' she slurred, still waving her arms above her head as if she was performing a rain dance.

'I believe it is *Grease!*' she cried delightedly. She took an elongated gulp of her wine before standing up, executing an exaggerated bow as the twins cheered gleefully for her.

My mother staggered back to her seat on the floor besides my dad who attempted to give her a high five, but they both completely missed one another's hands. I rolled my eyes and giggled.

'What?' she looked up at me sternly whilst tucking her short, blonde hair behind her ears. Her exorbitant sparkling diamonds dazzled against her pasty skin.

'Nothing' I snapped. *Here we go again.* I stared straight into her bright, blue eyes. She glared daggers back at me.

'Well, don't laugh at me then, laughing at people doesn't do well for their self-esteem does it?' she snarled.

'Your self-esteem could never be damaged, mum,' I retorted sarcastically.
With that remark she briskly stood up, tipping her glass of wine to the side so that it spilt on her deep purple dress, 'now look what you've made me do!' she screamed.

'Claire! She didn't do anything,' Veronica jumped in. Her villous eyebrows tightened on her face.

'Stay out of it, Ron! She always ruins everything!' she huffed, stamping her feet like a turbulent child, 'I'm sick of you and you're horrible comments. After everything we have done for you!' She cried, stomping out of the room. The clicks of her heels echoed throughout the house.

'Brookie, please don't argue with mummy, not on Christmas day,' Ruby pleaded in a high pitched whine.

'Don't listen to her, darling.' Veronica comforted as she placed herself next to me. Her long fingers brushed up and down my arm reassuringly, 'and don't you worry about it either you two, go and play with your new toys before bed time!' she ordered, nodding her head to my uncle.

Jeremy immediately jumped up from his seat, 'The tickle monster orders you to play with your toys!' he roared as he chased them in a circle. They soon forgot about my mother's outburst. I wished it could be that easy for me.

'I'm not, when do I ever listen to her?' I turned my attention back to auntie Veronica who was watching me worryingly.

My dad looked up at me with a disappointed expression painted across his un-ironed face, 'Go and apologise to your mother,' he ordered.
'Are you joking? I didn't do anything wrong!' I hissed so that the twins wouldn't hear. I promptly stood up, towering over him as he still lounged on the floor, 'she can't handle her drink.'

'If you are going to be disrespectful, then you can get out. She's right, we have put up with too much from you and you can't even give us a break on Christmas day!'

I looked down at my father sympathetically. Ignoring he's desperate attempt to disquiet me I lumbered into the hallway, shivering as my shorn feet met the bleak temperature of the marble flooring. My hair faintly patted against the bottom of my spine as I did so. I grabbed my coat off of the rangy coat hook before swiftly leaving the now very tense house. I knew there was a reason I hadn't joined in on the drinking, it was so I could escape.

I relaxed into the soft chair of my *BMW* and breathed in a huge sigh of relief. I was abhorred with the constant feud between my parents and me. I couldn't for the life of me think of anything I had done to them that was as terrible as they repay me with. It used to just be my mother that acted like the spawn of Satan, but recently my father had began to chime in. I knew that my mushy, lovey-dovey dad was only trying to 'stick up' for my mum, but it wasn't a good look for a man of nearly 55.

As I cruised down the countryside roads I contemplated what to do about the situation. Although I pondered this a lot, I never seemed to find a conclusion. I switched on the radio and flicked through the channels until I eventually found a channel reporting the news. The polished voice of the news reporter interrupted the conversation between the car engine and silence of the night time.

'…thank you, John. And if you want to get involved in John's bee charity so that they do not become extinct by 2020 then visit our website,' I rolled my eyes and leant towards the button to scan through the channels again, *'and in other news the remains of an unknown woman have been accidentally dug up by a group of young palaeontologists. Here's Rupert with the details.'*
I leant back in the chair and listened to the news report as I studied the road ahead of me, trying to determine where I had transported myself too. *'…The remains seem to be around 20 years old so police are currently looking at all cold cases and testing to see if there is any DNA or trace that can help them find out who this woman is. It has been confirmed that they are treating this as a murder case due to suspicious markings on the woman's remains. There will be more updates on this story as soon as we receive new information.'*

I knew there was only one place to go, so I steered the car in the direction of Jamie's, knowing that she too was probably having a miserable Christmas.

'Hello there, fitty!' Jamie giggled childishly as she glanced up to the television I had just switched on, looking up at the news channel I noticed there was a posh, balding man in a grey suit that seemed as though he was executing a speech, but he had been interrupted by a young boy who was shouting riotously at what looked like a member of the man's security team standing powerfully behind him.

'Thanks for letting me crash here, babe.' I sighed, thankful that I didn't have to spend the rest of Christmas with my brat of a mother.

As I positioned myself comfortably on Jamie's feathery mattress I studied the TV.
The security man had moved in front of the bald man to protect him as he was escorted from the scene, he began to seem tense and worried. His firm position did not change-yet his facial expression looked panicked, but not shocked I noticed. I wondered if he knew the boy.

 Suddenly, some police stepped in-pulling the boy to the ground. His brown curly hair bounced as they tackled him to the concrete. He managed to pull his head up far enough to look at the camera. His big, brown eyes were the only thing I noticed. At that moment the screen flickered and then the news reporters were on the screen explaining a slight technical hitch.

'Wonder what that was about,' I muttered to myself.

'He is probably stoned or something,' Jamie replied quietly as she hunched on the floor, delicately painting her perfectly square toe nails a deep ruby colour.

'No, I think there's more to that. He seemed really upset,' I pondered.

Jamie rolled her eyes, 'you're so dramatic,' she snapped before changing the subject, '*anyway,* you're very welcome. Thank god that we have each other right, B? Otherwise this Christmas would have been like any other day,' her bold eyes rolled dramatically again as she spoke.

'At least one good thing came of our families being total failures,' I agreed. Jamie's parents were on another extravagant holiday, celebrating Christmas together and leaving Jamie, yet again, at home alone.

Jamie laughed, 'one year we will be in our own homes, with our own families, you never know, I might be married to Harry,' she winked.

'Remind me, which one is Harry again?' I frowned; I couldn't keep up with her numberless queue of good-looking men.

'Harry, the guy from the fair, we went on a date the other night,' she snapped, 'keep up, B'

'Asking me to keep up with the amount of men you open your legs for is not an easy task Jamie,' I retorted.

Jamie wasn't offended easily, but that comment touched a nerve, just like I knew it would, 'EXCUSE ME?' she screamed, 'you can be such a bitch, B. And not that it's any of your business, but I haven't slept with him, we've been on ONE date, just because the only time you get any is when you go to get mental help don't take it out on me! Daniel is a head case too!'

'Too? What do you mean by *too?* I don't go for mental help, I go counselling, it's nothing to be ashamed of. Maybe you need some counselling, shall I book you in? Can you get off of your knees for 5 minutes to go to a counselling session with me?' I exclaimed.

This wasn't a rare occurrence, us two arguing over petty nonsense. We knew how to dig where it hurt, Jamie's weak spot was being seen as a slag, and mine was being seen as a nutter.

Jamie creased over laughing, 'that was a good one,' she howled, 'anyway, that's enough now, it's Christmas, Jesus Christ, peace and love and all that crap.'
'Merry fucking Christmas' I exhaled wistfully. Maybe this would be my motto for the foreseeable future.

'How was your Christmas?' Daniel asked.

I laughed, 'now we do the small talk?'

'No, I want to know,' he smiled, rolling over to face me. We were lying in his king sized bed, the sheets intertwined between our bodies and the pillows had been thrown somewhere on the floor. He tucked a strand of my now very messy hair behind my ear, as if that was going to help.

'My Christmas was tedious and uneventful,' I sighed, sitting up and throwing his large t-shirt on to cover myself up, 'what about yours?'

He rolled onto his back and pulled me on top of him, 'tedious and uneventful?' he chuckled 'you are a funny one. My Christmas was delightful actually.'

I looked down at his face as he spoke. His smile irritated me. You see, his mouth was stupidly enlarged, so whenever we actually spoke to each other I just wanted him to stop talking.

'Shut up,' I smiled as he was droning on about his Christmas dinner, clearly very passionate about the roast potatoes he's great aunt whatever her name is had served.
'Yes m'am' he replied, pulling me down to kiss him. Yes, I did realise that he said things like 'yes m'am' and yes, I did think everything that came out of that stupidly large mouth of his was also much like my Christmas, very tedious. But I didn't call him dreamy Daniel for no reason.

Dreamy Daniel was, well, very, very, very dreamy. And that I thought was a good enough reason as any to carry on stringing along my counsellor's receptionist.

January
The week I'd had off for Christmas was filled with drunken nights in Jamie's living room and days spent under Daniel's covers-so not too different from my usual day to day occurrences really.

I had resumed work on New Year's Day and it was like I had never left. I repeated the same routine. My day would start by leaving my very tense household before anyone was awake, then I'd sit in the stuffy trainee's office undertaking mundane paper-work while engaging in pointless trivial chatter with the new apprentices for most of the day. Lastly, at 7.30pm I would practically run out of the office doors and spend my evenings out with Jamie and a few of her friends, until I knew that everyone would be asleep at home and it was clear to go back.

Mr. Daniels had informed us in a back to work briefing that Mr. Spence had finally been located and they were close to bringing him in.

Harriet had still not returned to work, or any of my calls for that matter. Now that I didn't have Harriet to pass the time it had become rather boring sitting by that desk day after day with no real work to do. I guess I had thought that when I applied for this apprenticeship it would involve a lot more action and a lot less sitting around doing all of the report writing and making countless cups of coffees.

Through all of the boredom I had begun to look out of the big windows onto the busy road below and observe what everyone else was doing with their lives. I was thankful that I overlooked the street as it kept me occupied when everyone else in the office would be speaking utter nonsense.
It was late January and the weather was as bleak as it had been since October. I would watch as the unbelievably tall man with his well groomed looking dog would appear from the housing estate on the corner every morning at around 9AM. I'd named him Vladimir, Vladimir the giant, and decided that he'd previously worked in the circus before becoming a normal citizen.

After I returned from my lunch break at about 1:30pm the crazy running lady would 'jog' past. Her curly hair flailing around in the wind along with her arms, the only way I could describe her run was how Phoebe ran in *Friends*.

Then there was the bus load of obnoxious secondary school children that would spill out onto the path at around 3:45pm. The girl's skirts were rolled so far up that they may as well have not bothered wearing them, the boys would shout at them and they would giggle like, well like a bunch of school children.

Eventually, every evening without fail, a boy would sit down on a crooked bench placed next to the bus stop on the other side of the busy main road. He sometimes turned up around 7, other times he would just be sitting down as I was driving away.

He would always be wearing a green coat and jeans. He watched everyone and everything that went past him, like he was searching for something. I thought at first he was just waiting for the bus, but it would pass him each time. Then I thought maybe it was a girlfriend, or a friend, but no one ever showed. I couldn't quite think of a scenario for him just yet.

'How was work?' Mum asked me as I stepped into her car. My car was still at Jamie's from the night before where I had been too drunk and had to pay for a cab home. Luckily mum was passing by to pick the twins up from dance lessons so I had convinced her to pick me up-surprised that she'd agreed.

My eyes were blurry as a result of sitting in front of a computer all day, typing up reports that my Mr. Daniels had kindly asked me to copy up.

'Boring, like always,' I muttered doing up my seat belt and resting my head back breathing a huge sigh of relief that the day was done and the weekend was here.

'Maybe you shouldn't go in with a hangover and it wouldn't be that bad. Do you not care about your future? Because I'm telling you now, Brooke you are not staying at home until your 30 being a drunken wreck, because that's the way you're going' she nagged, switching on the ignition.

'Thank you for picking me up, but maybe we shouldn't talk,' I replied as I turned on the radio.
Mum leant over and slammed the button to turn off the radio. Her long, fake nails scratched against the metal, 'listen to me, Brooke. Don't go showing your boss what you're really like and getting sacked!'

'What I'm *really* like? What's that supposed to mean?' I rubbed my head as it began to pound increasingly with every word.

'You're a stupid, selfish cow. If you show them what you're really like then they will fire you straight away, trust me. Get out!' Mum shouted.

'What?' I laughed, bewildered by her behaviour yet again.

'You heard me, get out!' She leaned across me and opened the door.

'I am not just *getting out* I have nowhere to go do I?' I attempted to refuse as I jolted upwards in my seat, 'this is like an hour's walk from home and it's like the fucking Antarctic out here!'

Mum starred at me for a second-her eyes filled with hate-before slapping me viciously around the face, 'get out,' she ordered.

'Fine!' I shouted taking my seatbelt off and jumping out of the car. I was in shock; she had never laid a hand on me before.

My bag was violently thrown after me, 'you're rude and horrible and I've had enough! Do not think of coming home ever again!' she screamed.
I slammed the door in her face and stood there helplessly for a second or two, I watched as mum pulled her bright white Range Rover out of the turning and sped down the road without a second thought.

I waited a minute before crossing the road to sit down on the bench opposite work. I lounged there for what must have been about 10 minutes, pondering to myself about what to do for the night. Jamie was at work so I didn't want to bother her and all of the other people I knew were more like acquaintances, they wouldn't be people I could call for a place to crash. I scrolled through my phone and sighed, dreamy Daniel it was, I sent him a text asking if he wanted to meet up.

As I sent the text a boy sat down next to me; I tried to act like I hadn't acknowledged him and carried on looking at the cars going past, placing my phone back in my coat pocket. A strong smell of sweet aftershave blew my way in the wind, forcing me to sneeze.

'Bless you,' he smiled kindly. I looked at him-only quickly- but I noticed the same green coat I had seen sitting on this bench for the last couple of weeks.

I wondered why he was so late to take his seat today-it was already nearly 8pm. Thoughts ran through my head of whom or what could have held him up. I wanted to ask him why he always came to this spot, why is it so special? What does it mean to him?

'Thank you,' I blushed realising I'd probably left a bit of an awkward silence. I studied his face closely; he was rather beautiful in an un-groomed kind of way.

'Yeah you do,' He muttered.
'Excuse me?' I questioned.

'You do recognize me, mad boy from the news,' he rolled his eyes sarcastically and chuckled, 'that's what my mates keeps calling me,' he spoke in a strong cockney accent, I liked it.

'Oh no, I didn't recognise you from there but now that you come to mention it...' I replied, vaguely remembering the news report a month ago where the curly haired boy had been rugby tackled to the floor by the police. I wanted to ring Jamie and tell her I told her so, I knew there was an intriguing story to him, 'I recognise you more from the fact you sit here every night though,' I stated bravely, taken aback by my confidence.

He grinned, 'so being on the news for 15 seconds makes you famous enough to have a stalker then?' he joked.

'Oh, ha-ha. Don't flatter yourself,' I grinned back, 'I've just seen you around here a lot, what are you doing here?' I insisted. I couldn't help myself, I felt like I needed to know this strangers deal. Why was he acting like that on live TV? Does it have anything to do with why he never misses a night of sitting on this very uncomfortable little bench? I shifted in my seat. The night was becoming cold and I had been sitting in the same position for a while now.

'I could ask you the same thing, young girl sitting here on a Friday night,' He looked as though he was fighting to keep his warm, chestnut eyes from closing. Why was he so exhausted? I wondered again.

'Young? We're probably the same age,' I pointed out, 'I was just sitting here thinking of something to do tonight.'

He smiled crookedly, 'come up with anything yet?'
'Nope,' I sighed. I watched as he pulled out a cigarette box from his deep pocket, pointing it towards me, 'yeah, go on then,' I shrugged, *why not*? I thought to myself. I took one out of the box and the lighter from his hand and our cold fingers brushing up against each other briefly. I coughed as I took a long pull, it had been a while. This seemed to amuse him, I noticed that he had a nice smile; it made me feel at ease. I studied him further, he was dressed head to toe in dilapidated clothes, yet he managed to look rather handsome. Realising that I'd probably been starring at him for a little too long I turned away, taking another long pull of the cigarette.

'My name's Liam, by the way. What's yours?' he looked up at me with an intrigued look painted across his face. Smoke whirled out of his mouth like a snake emerging from the grass.

'Brooke,' I replied as I flicked some ash onto the cracked pavement. The cold breeze whistled past and I watched as the ash flew into the air, landing a few feet away from us in the middle of the road.

Liam didn't answer; he just chastely stared at me for a while, 'what?' I laughed, patting my iced face with my numbed hands to check there wasn't something there.

'Nothing,' his cheeks flushed red as he swiftly looked away, shaking his head as if he was cringing at himself. I dropped the cigarette onto the floor and stubbed it out with my burnished shoe. I shifted slightly closer to him as he turned back around to face me.

We stayed seated on the bench for some time; we spoke like we had known each other for years. I told him about how I loved to read books at night before bed and go for runs in the morning as they both relaxed me. I told him about how I loved animals, but was never allowed any growing up.

'Yeah, I used to spend my weekends in the pet shop round the corner. The owner would let me stay there all day petting the animals. All I had to do was help her feed them and stuff,'

'So she basically made you work and didn't pay you,' he laughed.

'Spending a day with puppies? Is that not better than getting paid?' I argued my case.

Liam told me about his love for films, especially romance. This fact surprised me as he didn't give off the film geek vibe at first. He boasted that he knew all of the famous quotes from any film, old and new.

'I have a room in my house that's just filled with DVD's and old videos' he admitted.

'Videos,' I chuckled, 'you still have a video player?'

'Yep, how else am I going to watch the first couple of Harry Potter's?' he replied seriously.

'Buy them on DVD?' I laughed.

'Not the same,' he replied adamantly, 'it just wouldn't be the same listening to Hagrid say *you're a wizard Harry* on a DVD. It just wouldn't.'

I giggled. Usually I wouldn't even talk to a stranger, I would have stood up and walked away the minute he had acknowledged my existence, but not once did we speak about work, or family, or anything of the sort. He was just interested in *me*. He asked me about what I loved to do and what songs I played on repeat, what my thoughts were on aliens and what my favourite food was. It had been a very long time since I'd had a real conversation like that.

'God, we've been here for so long,' I stated as I noticed the time change to 8:50pm on my watch under the dim street light towering above us, 'I should probably get going, find somewhere to go tonight,' I sighed, remembering that I wasn't welcome back home.

He nodded as he tightened another cigarette between his lips. I watched as the flame from his lighter lit up his tanned face, 'can I ask you something?' he frowned as he leant back into his seat placing the lighter back into his coat pocket.

'Of course,' I answered hesitantly, wrapping my arms tighter round myself to protect my hands from the brisk wind that was gushing past. At that moment my phone started to ring, it was Daniel.

'Do you want to come with me?' Liam asked, I looked down at Daniel's name lighting up my phone and then back up at Liam's ruggedly handsome face, 'or do you need to answer that?' the way he asked me was so calm, so reassuring, so intriguing, I couldn't say no. His dark eyes starred at me, his long, thick eyelashes almost looked as if they were weighing them down.

I declined the call and switched my phone to silent. 'I don't need to answer that.'
I took a few pulls on the cigarette he had just passed to me and watched as he stood up and held out his hand. I noticed how tall he was, he transcended over me and I felt almost inclined to take his hand and follow wherever he wanted me to go. I blew out cigarette smoke slowly as I stood up, but through the mist I saw a smile.

It was so out of character for me, to follow a stranger to an unknown location, to not be suspicious or think they have ulterior motives. But the way he spoke, the way he laughed, the countless stories he told me as I followed him unknowingly along the winding paths he led me down made me want to stay, I wanted to know more.

We reached a shadowy high street that I didn't recognise, there were a few flickering bar signs and a group of giggly girls staggering arm in arm past us.

'Liam!' a deep voice called from ahead, I could make out a faint figure under the neon light of what looked to be a club. He didn't look to be much taller than Liam. As we drew closer I noticed a group of boys, all had dark, untidy hair and kind smiles, none of them as bewitching as Liam's.

'This is Brooke,' Liam proudly presented me to the group, 'we just met, but I'm gonna marry 'her, one day' he joked, winking at me. I melted a little bit inside.
We entered a building which was entirely decorated with brick walls and shabby leather chairs, the music was deafening. The boys ushered me to the crummy looking bar and bought me a drink straight away, they seemed to know all of the bar staff and addressed them by nicknames, so I assumed this was a regular night for Liam and his gang. I caught my reflection in the mirrored wall of the bar and realized that I was still dressed in my smart, un-exciting work clothes.

I popped open a few buttons of the white shirt I had tucked into some high-wasted black trousers, my lace bra slightly revealed itself in my now lowered top, I unclipped my unkempt hair from the messy bun perched carelessly on top of my head and shook subtly so that my long, chocolate locks fell over the ridge of my breasts and down to my waist, I caught Liam gazing at me intensely as I took a large gulp of my red wine, a feeling I didn't recognise surged through me as my eyes met his. Maybe it was excitement or maybe it was danger, I wasn't sure, but I liked it.

'So Brooke,' one of Liam's friends shouted over the loud music at me, 'how do you know Liam?'

'We met a few hours ago,' I laughed, studying the slightly chubby, very spotty boy that was talking to me, 'what about you?'

'We all go way back, primary school,' he replied, gulping down some more beer, his breath stunk strongly of alcohol and cigarettes.

'Dale, what are you saying to her,' Liam's rasping voice questioned from behind me, he lightly placed his hands around my waist and lent forwards until I could feel his warm breath tickle the back of my neck, 'I don't usually ask random girls from the street out, just wanted to let you know,'

I turned to face him, his hands still held their place around me, 'I'd be worried if you did,' I smiled, 'bit weird,'

'I'm glad I asked you though, random girl from the street,' he smirked.

'Thank you, random boy from the bench outside my work,' I laughed.

Liam swiftly released his grip, 'you work there?'

'Don't panic, I'm not a police officer or anything, I'm just training in the NCA at the moment, I'm quite new to it all really,' I paused as I watched him study me intently, 'oh, are you like a criminal or something?' I took a step back, but immediately relaxed as he laughed and pulled me back towards him.

'No, I'm not a criminal or something, I'm just impressed,' he reassured me, 'you're getting better and better by the minute,' he added.

'Oh, well thanks,' I blushed.

He laughed at my reaction, 'so when you're done training do you get a police officer's uniform to wear?' he prodded teasingly. I rolled my eyes and ignored the question, taking a swig of my wine instead. 'Okay, random girl from the street, how would you feel about going on a date with me?'

'I guess that would be okay,' I smiled as I shrugged my shoulders casually. Inside I was anything but casual.

'You didn't mention anything about the uniform?' he prodded again.

'You don't need to be a police officer to have a uniform,' I winked, turning around and walking towards the bar to get myself another large wine. *That was such a Jamie line* I muttered to myself, she would be so proud.

It was around 3AM and Camden Town was closing its bars for the night. I felt a wave of disappointment rush over me as I was having such a good time. It was like the shy, anxious girl I had always been disappeared around Liam and his group of friends. Maybe this was what Dr. Daw had meant when she said 'being around the right people will send you on the right path.' I'd always thought she spoke in such riddles, but maybe it was just because I hadn't yet experienced the things she was describing.

Liam grabbed my hand and pulled me back along the street, 'come with me?' he slurred drunkenly.

'Where are we going now?' I whispered as he gently pulled me along. His friends were walking in the opposite direction waving and shouting goodbye to us.

'My favourite spot in the city,' he grinned widely. He seemed as though everything in the world fascinated and excited him. I wondered for a moment what it would be like to see the world through his rose tinted spectacles, it must have been nice.

I followed him back down the street for a while until we walked through a village like area. Liam clutched my hand and sighed.

'Primrose Hill,' he stated as we turned the corner.

'This is a good spot,' I said as we took our place at the very top of the hill which overlooked the beautiful lit up city that I called home. I slumped myself down on the floor next to him and took in the sparkling surroundings.

'Isn't it?' He smiled, seemingly happy that I approved of his favourite place. 'When a man is tired of London he is tired of life,'

'I don't know what film that's from?' I frowned, remembering what he had said about constantly quoting films.

'Not a film, Samuel Johnson wrote that.' He continued as he looked at my blank expression, 'he was a writer, don't know much of his stuff but I always remember that quote because it's so true.' I watched in awe as Liam rambled on about writers and poets and films. His lust for life was truly contagious. 'Sorry, I talk a lot,' he apologized.

'Don't be sorry,' I giggled, 'I like listening to people who actually have something to say you know?'

He nodded in agreement, 'here's a question.' He turned to face me crossing his legs and cupping my hand in his. 'If you had to die, like there was no other choice but to die, how would you want to go?'

I pulled my hand away, 'are you about to murder me? Because this has gone from a really good night to the start of a horror film really quickly,' I laughed nervously.

'No, no. I'm not going to murder you. I promise,' he smirked.

Our eyes lingered longingly for a few seconds before I slowly lay down onto the damp, cold grass. 'I guess, if I had to, I'd go in my sleep. Peaceful, not knowing what was happening, I guess that's the least horrific way of dying.' I answered. 'What about you?' I turned to face him as he lay down next to me.

He thought for a second and then his big, brown, beautiful eyes widened. 'I'd want to die a hero. I'd want to die for a cause or for the people I loved. I'd want my last seconds to be so filled with love and purpose, you know?' he paused and tilted his head to face me, 'I'd want to die for a reason and not just slip away unknowingly, no offence,' he finished.

'None taken,' I chuckled. 'That is a very heroic way of dying, I commend you.'

He tilted his head to face me, 'was that a bit of a depressing question to ask a complete stranger?'

'No, it's very insightful. The answer says a lot about a person, I might ask it more.' I reassured him as I looked up at the stars.

There was him, a person who would die for the people he loved and then there was me, a person who most days wanted to close her eyes and slip away peacefully. Two complete opposites, but somehow the universe had made it so that in that exact moment we were laying next to each other under the stars. It was the first night for as long as I could remember that I didn't want to close my eyes and I didn't want to sleep because reality was actually a lot better. I knew once the sun rose that my mundane life would take its toll again, but in that moment I was extremely happy that I'd met this beautiful stranger with the curly hair.

'It's been very nice meeting you, Brooke.' Liam breathed as he felt for my hand in the darkness, 'I think this is the beginning of a beautiful friendship.'

'Casablanca?' I guessed as he grinned up at the sky.

February

It was the morning of my 24th birthday and I was awoken by the sound of Jamie's phone buzzing against her pillow, much like every morning since I had been staying at her house.

Her parents had been home for a couple of days after their Christmas trip, but they would travel for work for the majority of each year, leaving Jamie to have free run of the house.

I smiled as I reminisced on all the times we had slept in her bedroom as children, playing with dolls and sharing our secrets, there were photos of her and I all around the room. I checked my phone for any messages, I sighed as there was one from my mum, I guessed that it probably wasn't a message wishing me a happy birthday, and I was right.

I meant it when I said that you are not allowed back, you do not realize how unhappy and on edge you make everyone and the last week has been so good without you there. The twins are much happier and so are me and your dad. I will let you know when we are all going to be out and you can collect your stuff and leave your key on the side. You are not welcome here. Until I get an apology for your behavior lately I do not want to hear a word from you, none of us do. Have fun partying and drinking yourself to death.

My eyes filled with tears, but not because I was upset, out of anger. I looked up at Jamie fast asleep in her bed and then scrolled down my phone at my other messages. There was one from Liam, finally. I hadn't heard from him all week, I'd also been covering the earlier shifts at work, which meant I didn't get my nightly fix of staring at him from the window.

How has your week been? Do you want to do something today? X

Liam stood in the doorway of the bus that had just stopped next to me, 'come on, I've paid for your ticket already' he ushered.

I climbed inelegantly up the steps and followed him to the seats at the back, I noticed he was dressed a bit smarter than the last time I had seen him, but he still wore the infamous green coat, 'you going somewhere nice?' I asked, studying his ensemble of black skinny jeans and a tight white shirt.

'Yeah, we both are,' he smiled knowingly.
I had never experienced meeting such a mysterious person before. Everyone nowadays is so quick to tell you their life story and plaster everything on social media; it was exciting to meet someone of whom I knew nothing about. I peered out of the bus window as we passed trees stripped bare of their leaves due to the harsh winter, I felt empathy. I too felt like I have been stripped bare over the course of my life. I wanted to start fresh, bloom into something new.

'Are you sure you're okay girl?' he asked, touching my leg only for a second, but a second was long enough to send another rush of excitement through my body. I didn't realise I was making my emotional state so obvious, I needed to put a smile on my face and forget about my intolerable mother for good.

'Yeah of course, nothing out of the ordinary,' I lied. He seemed to accept my answer for the moment as he didn't reply.

A few stops later, Liam jumped up and grabbed my hand, tilting his head for me to follow him, 'where are we going?' I giggled as we exited the bus; Liam pulled me along a small cobbled street.

He weaved his way out of hurrying shoppers and I laughed nervously as I tried to stay with him. After a few more minutes of being blindly led to another one of Liam's destinations, he swiftly stopped and pulled me towards him, my heart started beating faster and the hairs on the back of my neck stood up.

He paused for only a second; searching my face for a reaction, the tension between our close bodies filled the air like smoke souring out of a bonfire. He grinned and as I looked into his big, brown eyes, I knew in that moment that I was well and truly fucked. Locking his hand tighter around mine he led me into the pub that I hadn't even noticed we were standing next to, the warmth hit me as soon as we entered, along with the smell of delicious food and strong beer.

'Liam!' a woman's voice called. A petite, glossy, black haired woman emerged from behind the bar. She was wearing an apron over a short, ebony dress and effortlessly carrying a drinks tray, 'hello stranger!' she smiled warmly.

'Katrina,' he nodded politely, 'this is Brooke,' he held me around the waist.

'Oh, you didn't tell me you had a girlfriend, Liam?' she winked at me.

'Oh no…' I began to correct her, but Liam butted in.

'Yes, beautiful isn't she?' he smiled at her, looking at me with a soppy look in his eyes.

'Aw! Go sit in the corner and I will get you the menu babe,' she cooed over him as she strutted off back behind the bar.

'What was that all about?' I hissed as he led me over to the table.

'Just play along, they do a couple's discount on a weekend,' he whispered, waving at some old, bearded men crowded around a small booth in the corner, all drinking big glasses of beer.

'Oh,' I chuckled, but felt slightly disappointed, hearing someone refer to me as their girlfriend was actually rather nice, I'd never had one before.

'My lady,' he grinned as he pulled my chair out and bowed.

Katrina wiggled back over and handed us both a menu, 'couples weekend discount, ten percent off of the main menu. How are you doing anyway babe?' she asked, perching herself on the empty table beside us.

'I'm good, how you been?' he smiled, opening the menu and placing it on the table. I fidgeted nervously in my chair as I listened to their conversation.

'*Very* good, which you'd know if you'd been to see me recently! I'm engaged!' she giggled, flashing off a big diamond ring on her hand.

'Aw, congratulations! Who is he?' he asked as he held her hand and examined the glistening diamond for a few second.

'Congratulations,' I smiled shyly.

Katrina smiled at me before continuing her conversation with Liam, I got the impression that they had known each other for a very long time. 'Oh, no one you know. You need to meet him. George would have liked him,' she said somberly.

'Oh well, didn't you say she liked any man?' Liam joked.

'Yes, she did indeed,' Katrina giggled, 'I'll leave you two to it, call me over when you're ready to order!'

'Who's George?' I asked nosily as I read through the traditional pub menu.

'My mum,' he smiled at me, 'her and Katrina were good friends, my mum used to work here actually, before I was born.'

'Oh right, where does she work now then?' I questioned again.

'She died,' he looked up at me, still smiling as if to reassure me that he was fine.

'Oh, I'm so sorry,' I reached out and grabbed his hand.

'Brooke, it's fine,' he reassured me, squeezing my hand; 'it was a long time ago, I promise I will tell you everything, but not now, I'm meant to be cheering you up.'

'You don't have to tell me,' I smiled reassuringly at him, 'and cheering me up, there's nothing wrong?' I insisted again.

'Brooke, I don't know you well, but I can tell when someone's got something on their mind,' he frowned.

'Maybe you know me a lot better than you think then,' I sighed.

He gazed into my eyes intensely for what seemed like quite a while, still clutching hold of my hand; 'Maybe...' he finally replied.

The clicks of Katrina's heels interrupted the moment and I quickly released my grip of Liam's hand.

'Have you decided what you two are having yet?' she asked.

Liam nodded at me to go first, 'Er, yeah, I will have the full English breakfast with a side of onion rings and large chips, and then for dessert I will have the sticky toffee pudding with custard, and can I have a large coke with it please?' as I looked up from the menu I noticed that Liam and Katrina were staring at me in awe, 'what?' I asked, confused.

'How are you so skinny? I have to eat like a rabbit to look like this.' she laughed, quickly jotting down what I had just ordered.

'Well I was just going to order a sandwich, but I'll have the same as her,' Liam grinned at me.

The 'date' succeeded in cheering me up and I left the pub that night in a much greater mood than the one I had entered it in. After devouring our food we stayed long into the evening, the group of weathered men told us all about their time in the army and navy and how they love to spend their retired days fishing, a lot of jokes about moaning wives waiting for them at home were made too.

Katrina's fiancé popped in to see her and we listened to the many romantic stories about how they had met and how he proposed. Liam's eyes lit up at this point, I was surprised at how much he really did *love* romance.

As the night went on and everyone had probably drunk way more than they had intended to, the karaoke machine was switched on and I ended up doing the a few duets with a friendly and very drunk fisherman named William, I couldn't remember the last time I had laughed so much.
I walked out of the tiny pub door, still laughing as the cold wind of the winter's night hit me like a ton of bricks.

Liam wrapped his large, green coat around my shoulders and led me back up the narrow street, 'this is my favourite thing about you,' I stated.

'What, my tatty old coat?' he laughed in amusement, 'don't have much going for me then do I?' he added.

I giggled, 'I just mean it's so you. You couldn't wear another coat it would be weird.'

He laughed at my drunken statement. 'I can't believe you didn't tell me it was your birthday!' he sighed, 'I would have got you something.'

'You don't need to get me anything, my own family haven't even got me a card,' I glanced at him as he put his arm around my shoulders. He took the bus with me and walked me to Jamie's front door.

'Thank you,' I slurred, 'I had a good time.' He chuckled, tucking a lose strand of my hair that was blowing in the wind behind my ear before leaning around me to knock gently on the door.

'Oh hey birthday girl, where have you been hiding?' Jamie laughed as she opened the door and pulled me inside, 'you look a right state,'

'Wait, your coat' I murmured, looking back over my shoulder to hand it back to Liam, but the mysterious brown eyed stranger had slipped away into the darkness, once again leaving me breathless.

The sound of my phone alarm the next morning rudely awoke me from my slumber; I squinted at the clock, 5:00 AM was staring up at me very brightly, I pressed the snooze button and fell onto my back again; I wanted a few extra minutes in the cosy spare bedroom of Jamie's large home to prepare myself for the long day ahead.

I crept out of the door at around six; being careful not to wake Jamie up on her only day off. My headache was almost unbearable, I sighed as I recalled the events of the night before and how I longed to be back with Liam already. I walked slowly to the bus stop with my shoulder bag gently thumping against my leg, Liam's coat draped tightly over my crossed arms. There was no way I was attempting to drive to work after how much alcohol I had consumed.

The crisp morning air was blowing my long pony tail over my shoulder, little strands of hair hitting the side of my face. The street was just waking up; birds chirped in the trees, a few curtains twitched as nosy neighbours looked out of their windows, an old lady in her dressing gown was standing outside her chipped, red door-pursing a cigarette between her lips while searching for something in her pockets.

I unwillingly strolled through the steel rotating doors and into the bright blue reception that I was so familiar with. I walked across the hall to the front desk, deciding I wanted to find out if anyone knew where Harriet had disappeared to. Also I was trying to waste as much time before having to endure another day in the office.

'Hey Carla,' I greeted the middle aged woman tapping away on her computer behind the front desk.

'You're Brooke, right?' Carla pushed her glasses up her nose and smiled, 'how can I help?'

'Harriet, she was doing training with me, she hasn't been here for weeks and I was just wondering if she got moved to another place or something?'

The whole time I spoke, Carla tapped a pen annoyingly against the desk. 'I know another one of the trainees quit just before Christmas, maybe that could be her?'

'She wouldn't just quit,' I answered as I placed my bag on the desk to pull out my phone.

'Well I don't know I've never met the girl, boss man just told me that another one had bit the dust the other day. There will be none of you left soon, such a waste of resources and money, training people up for months just for them to quit and go and work in a corner shop…'

'…Mr. Daniels told you that?' I rudely interrupted, but Carla was known for holding people up at reception due to her mundane droning and I wasn't in the mood to be polite today.

'Yes, gorgeous isn't he?' she grinned, her pink cheeks flushing.

'I guess so' I murmured, 'that's weird that she would just quit, she loved it here,' I rummaged around in my bag but couldn't feel my phone in there, 'or not,' I sighed.
Reluctantly, I signed in and made my way towards the rusty lift in the far corner of the room. I repeated the same routine I always did daily, but this time instead of just noticing Liam walk to the bench, I found myself waiting for him to make his appearance *you're pathetic* I thought to myself as I swivelled around in my squeaky office chair, chewing on a pen and starring at the minutes go by on the loud wall clock above my head.

I decided to look into Liam's little TV appearance, I hadn't asked him about it as I didn't want to ruin the perfect picture I had created of him in my head, but I knew that there had to be something wrong, nobody was that perfect in real life.

After a few Google searches, a YouTube clip of the news report popped up, I watched closely as Liam appeared, screaming and swearing at the body guard standing in the background. He was an extremely scary looking man, his biceps were larger than my head and he had a horrendous scar running down the entire right side of his face.

Liam was shouting at the man, 'Guedo you coward, what did you do?'

'Guedo,' I whispered to myself, 'there can't be many people with that name,' I typed the name 'Guedo' into Google, hoping for a full Wikipedia page on the man, but all that appeared was meanings and interpretations of the name.

It seemed to be a slang term for Italian American's who conduct themselves in the way a mobster in a film would, I wondered if it was an ironic nickname he'd given himself, maybe it was a middle finger to the historically demeaning nature of the word.

I sighed; I couldn't find anything about Liam anywhere, no Facebook, no Instagram, no more news reports, just the video on you-tube and an old MySpace account from when he was about 11 years old.

At around 2pm we were called to the department's meeting room as some new evidence had come to light. I walked through the door and squeezed past bodies to reach the other side of the already filled up room. I placed myself in a chair that was next to some people who I knew were just as socially awkward as me and wouldn't try and spark up conversation. I nodded at them and gave them a slight smile before slouching down in the uncomfortable plastic chair.

'Right everyone!' Mr. Daniels' voice boomed over the buzz of conversation, everyone immediately took their seats; a few taller men leant across the wall at the back of the room clutching on to cups of steaming coffee.

'We seem to have had a break through at last!' he declared as he rolled in the old TV that was usually pushed to the back of the staff room. 'Here I have Mr. Andrew Spence's interview, conducted yesterday at 5:52pm. I want you all to watch and listen carefully, we have the bastard and now it's time to get the rest of them.'

Everybody watched the tape intensely, jotting down notes and gasping at some of the rude, derogatory things Andrew Spence was mumbling. He was defiant in revealing any information, insisting that his house was purely used as a place to hide the girls until they were shipped elsewhere.

'I never saw their faces,' he repeated for the thousandth time, 'everyone wore balaclavas, they would drop the girls to me and leave.'
'You say you have been working for this organisation for a long time, 3 years to be exact,' Katie, the lead investigator on this case stated as she tucked her short fiery hair behind her ears. 'In that time you must have heard something, seen something, just something little. Do you think you could remember *anything* at all that would help us, and more importantly help *yourself*?'

Katie studied his face closely as the wheels turned around in his brain. After a minute had passed she swiftly stood up from her chair and shrugged, 'well it looks like you are going to be behind bars for a very long time then Mr. Spence, you are the only person we have that is linked to these horrific crimes, crimes that will see you sent away for a lifetime. We have substantial evidence and DNA all over your home and witness statement after witness statement of the poor girls you have been holding there against their will. Without any other information, I believe we are done with you. Interview terminated at….'

Andrew interrupted her as he clearly began to panic, 'there is one thing,' he mumbled, jolting his eyes towards his lawyer who was shaking his head. 'They always said seven,'

'Seven?' Katie repeated, lowering herself back onto to her chair.

'Yeah, I remember now. Whenever they dropped the girls off they would always say something like, they will be here until seven collects. Seven must be the person in charge, right?'

At that moment Mr. Daniels stopped the tape and studied our faces. 'We must find out who seven is,' he stated as he stuck a post it note with the number 7 next to a question mark right in the centre of the board. 'I'm afraid that's all we have to go on until we can get some more out of Andrew Spence.'

At around 6:50pm-not that I was watching the time-I noticed Liam take his place on the same spot on his bench, pull out one cigarette from his pocket and spark it up. He stretched his legs out and lounged back into the bench. Like every other day. I glanced at his green coat I had hung on the back of the door, thankful that I had a conversation starter tonight.

I practically skipped out of the swivel doors and across the road when 7:30pm hit, but was disappointed to see that yet again, Liam had disappeared.

After a few days of Liam being a no show I began to question my sanity. Had I made this boy up? Had I seen him on the news and imagined him into 'real life?' I knew I was pretty messed up, but maybe I needed to see Dr. Daw again sooner rather than later. I kept his coat on the back seat of my car, just as a physical reminder that I wasn't losing my mind.

I went through the whole miserable week with no text messages and no sightings of Liam on his bench, until Friday came around. I stepped out of work and was more than relieved to see that he was waving at me from across the street, leaning against the bus stop with a cigarette held on top of his ear.

'You aright, girl?' Liam beamed that dangerously dreamy grin at me. His big eyes seemed to light up as he saw me and the harsh wind blew his curly locks across his face.

I stood awkwardly in front of him for a second as our eyes lingered intently at each other, 'so instead of sitting on that very uncomfortable little bench in the freezing cold shall we go somewhere warmer?' I broke the silence, surprised at my confidence.

'Sounds like a plan,' he winked.

I lead him across the street to my car. It was weird that I was leading him somewhere for a change. 'Alright miss BMW.' He raised his eyebrows at me as he relaxed into the passenger seat. 'You surprise me every day,'

'Why?' I laughed as I started the engine, the music I had been blaring through my speakers that morning boomed through the car making us both jump. Chris Brown was midway through singing the chorus to *back to sleep* and I blushed as I saw Liam's eyebrows rise even more.

'Sorry, I was feeling a type of way this morning,' I muttered as I turned down the volume and switched to a different playlist. Liam burst out laughing as some classical music played through the speakers. I tilted my head and smiled innocently, 'the real me is in fact, an angel.'

'Have you had a good week?' Liam smirked at me as I switched to a generic radio station.

'Same old,' I replied, 'Oh, you left without taking this with you the other night,' I added as I reached to the back seat and passed him his coat. I was going to miss driving with the strong smell of his aftershave filling my car.

After driving around for a while we pulled up at the cinema in Camden and after much deliberation decided that the only film worth seeing was Cold Pursuit starring Liam Neeson.

We sat at the back of the cinema like two teenagers, sharing popcorn and slurping on our Ice Blasts. Liam yawned and placed his arm around my shoulder halfway through the film which made me giggle a little bit too loud.

'*Shh*,' a podgy looking lady shot us a look from a few rows in front. I cupped my hand over my mouth as I tried not to laugh even more as Liam pulled a funny face at her in reply.

'Any quotes worth remembering from that film?' I asked Liam as we strolled out of the ODEON and back into the cold of the night. I shivered as I rushed towards the car park. 'That was an Oscar Wilde quote at the start, right?' I asked him as we flung ourselves into the car and quickly switched on the heater.

'Some cause happiness wherever they go, others whenever they go,' Liam answered, 'yeah that's a good one, noted.' He tapped his head with his finger. 'I had fun tonight, Brooke,' Liam added as yet again he stared deep into my eyes.

'So did I,' I smiled timidly, 'So, do you want to go home or…' I paused and looked at him.

'Or…' he winked. '…Or sounds good.'

'Hello B,' Jamie answered her door cheerfully, before laying eyes on Liam, '*and* B's friend,'

'Nice to meet you, heard a lot about you. I'm Liam,' he smiled politely.

'*Liam*,' she grinned and nodded at me, 'you two love birds coming in or you just gonna stand there?' she grinned, pulling on Liam's arm so he fell through the front door, 'I haven't heard *anything* about you, she's so secretive when it comes to boyfriends.'

I shook my head and laughed as I followed them into the house that was basically my home now, 'sorry J I left my door keys here this morning, again,' I laughed.

'So what are you doing here?' Jamie asked as she wiggled over to the kitchen and retrieved three bottles of beer from the fridge. I watched as Liam admired her bum in the very short pyjama bottoms she was wearing. I slapped his arm playfully as I sat down next to him on the sofa.

'I had a long day at work, then we went to the cinema, Liam was just…' before I had a chance to finish Jamie butted in, like always.

'…Liam was just here to keep you company,' she smirked as she passed us the opened bottles before falling down on an armchair.

'I was 4 when mum died,' Liam sniffed, taking a long pull of another cigarette and then passed it to me. Jamie had finally taken the hint that we wanted to be alone and had reluctantly stomped upstairs; I could hear the theme tune of *Keeping up with the Kardashians* from her open window.

Liam and I were perched on the back door step with a bottle of wine, a pack of cigarettes and the starry night sky as our only companions.

'She used to work where you work, when I was old enough to understand that mum was missing I used to walk there every day and sit outside hoping that I would see her, I suppose after a few years it just became habit.' Finally, I had an explanation to why he always sat on that bench.

'Then she got this boyfriend, I don't know how they met, I don't know anything really, I never really got a word she said about it, I was too young to understand,' he paused and smiled as if he was having a memory of her.

Although he was smiling, you could clearly see the pain in his eyes. 'I remember her coming home one day, *Liam baby, mummy's gonna be a rich bitch after this promotion!* I remember I was eating dinner, beans on toast. She always called me that, Liam baby,' he laughed.

'That's cute,' I smiled, 'she sounded lovely. What about your dad, was he not around to help you find her?' I realized I didn't really know much about Liam, for the number of things we had spoken about recently. I felt guilty for not knowing more.

'I never knew my dad, he left mum when he found out she was pregnant.' He replied matter-of-factly.

'Oh, I'm sorry,' I apologized softly, running out of things that I could say in response to his heartbreak.

'Don't be, I'm not,' he managed a smile, 'anyway, yeah, I guess she was working overtime, through the nights, early mornings, never really slept, I remember her never really being home,'

'But you were only young,' I whispered, not wanting to say anything bad about his mum, but I couldn't believe a 4 year old was left alone to fend for himself.

He shrugged in response to my comment before carrying on. 'I started doing some digging and found a few notes from work lying around the house, I just remember reading something about a Rebecca bird who worked with her, she was in a car crash or something and had been sent to jail. But apart from that it was all just cases they had been working on and it was all a bit depressing.'

'So that security guy on the news, that had something to do with your mum?' I asked carefully, not wanting to dig too deep and upset him, but I also really wanted to know who Guedo was.

'That was her boyfriend,' anger filled his voice and poured out into his beautiful eyes, 'I wouldn't be alone all the time, he was always lingering around, I remember a lot of shouting, mainly him shouting at her, her coming downstairs with bruises and blood over her, why she was with him I'll never understand, since she's been gone people always tell me about how many men were after her, like Katrina from the pub the other day. She said my mum could have had anyone she wanted, why Guedo, just why.'

I shook my head, I couldn't believe what I was hearing, and I thought I had it hard with my spoilt little brat problems, at least I had a mum.

'Mum was never late home from work; I think maybe she hated leaving me alone, but didn't have a choice. I had to walk with the neighbor kid who was older than me to and from school because she couldn't take me. One morning I woke up and mum was shouting up the stairs, *Liam baby,* see *you at normal time yeah? Mummy loves you.* And then that night, she never came home.'

'How did she die?' I asked quietly, not sure if I was over stepping the mark with my questions.

Liam didn't seem to care about my inquisitiveness as he answered without batting an eyelid. I wondered if he'd answered this question many times before, 'I don't know; no one has ever found her, no one even really knows I exist. I was only in the second year of school, funny thing is I carried on walking with the next door neighbor to school and back even after she'd gone, just because I thought that's what I had to do.'

'You were 4 and you used to get yourself ready and go to school?' I was shocked; I'd never heard anything like it.

'Yeah pretty much, Chris-that was the neighbour's name-used to come in and help me from what I remember, like in the mornings he would make me a packed lunch and stuff. He was there quite a lot because his mum and dad were druggies or something; he didn't really like being at home. He was only a few years older than me; we're still mates now actually. Then one of my mum's friends, Carlos, moved in with me once he had found me alone after a few weeks of her being gone. He just called school one day and told them I was moving, pretending he was my dad; I never went to another school again. I got a job when I was 12 with him at his garage, where I work now, and that's it really. I found out Guedo was gonna be working where that interview was happening the other month and went to confront him, didn't know there was gonna be so many cameras and the news there, but seeing him again after all these years made me so pissed off, I just went for him.'

'Oh,' I whispered, in shock at everything he had just disclosed. I'd never known anyone who had lived a life like him, 'and you've been trying to figure out what actually happened to her?'

'Yeah, I guess so. We always know what Guedo is up to; Carlos promised he'd never stop looking for her. I think deep down he loved her. But Guedo has been quiet for years, pops up in a news report or something here and there because his security firm caters for the rich people and the politicians. But yeah, we have never stopped looking for answers. ' Liam explained, looking down at his feet, he almost seemed ashamed.

I thought I was drawn to Liam because he was mysterious, but now that I knew more about him-I could feel myself falling even more. I wrapped my hands around his muscular arm and lent on his shoulder, not knowing what in the world I could say to comfort him in that moment.

Before we fell in love

After cancelling many sessions with Dr. Daw as of recent months, I felt as though I'd better show up for this one. As I walked in I noticed dreamy Daniel leaning against the vending machine, his ripped jeans rolled up around the ankles, and his loud shirt was tucked in on one side.

'The 1980's just called, they want their clothes back,' I shouted at him from across the room. A few chuckles echoed through the waiting area, Daniel's face lit up with pure glee. He leapt over the chair in front and spun me around in his arms.

I wondered why he'd had to leap over chairs and spin me around, why couldn't he just walk over to me and greet me like any normal human would. Then I thought that if Liam leapt over a chair to greet me I probably would have fainted on the spot, so maybe it only irritated me because Daniel was the wrong person.
'Hello you,' he leant down to kiss me, but without even thinking I stepped backwards, avoiding the kiss so obviously that I can imagine he wanted to turn back time and retract that move, 'well that's never happened before,' he laughed nervously, 'you alright?'

'Sorry, I'm fine. Just you know me and public displays of affection,' I laughed, playfully punching him on the arm. Oh wow, I forgot how big those arms were, I thought to myself. No, Brooke, you cannot do your counsellor's receptionist in the storage cupboard again, no matter how fit he is. I argued with my straying thoughts.

At that moment, Dr. Daw appeared from the ladies toilets.
'Oh hello there, Brooke,' she greeted me with a nod, 'would you like to come through,'

Thank god for that. I smiled, 'I'll see you soon, yeah?' I reassured him, giving him an awkward wave goodbye.

March

After nearly two weeks of constantly checking my phone and not hearing a word from Liam, or seeing him at his usual spot outside work, I had given up on the hope of finally having some excitement in my life; I had slid back in to the repetitious life I'd always lived, spending the weekdays in the same four walls of my unexciting office and spending most weekends and evenings getting drunk at Jamie's-which was now my permanent residence.

I had came to the conclusion that Liam had regretted opening up about his mum to me and thought it was best to stay away. I could understand, it must have been hard speaking to me knowing I worked in a place that his mum was probably last seen alive.

I hadn't heard from my parents since my mum's delightful text message on my birthday, I'd met with Auntie Veronica for coffee a few times, but I was quite content with not seeing my irritating family members for the time being. I had collected all of my stuff whilst they were out and moved into the spare room of Jamie's house. She was happy to have the company, and with my contribution towards the bills she didn't have to work so tirelessly to make ends meet.

It was a normal Friday evening, I had taken the same dreary road back from work and was listening to some *Shania Twain* in the bath, getting ready for another night of drinking and watching Jamie kiss strangers, when my phone buzzed loudly, there was no caller ID but I answered anyway.

'Hello?' I answered, placing my phone on the toilet seat next to the bath and pressing the loud speaker button.

'Hey, Brooke…' a familiar voice greeted me from the other end of the phone.

'Oh, Liam, hi…' my heart was in my throat, I sat up so fast in the bath I almost caused a tidal wave over the side.

'What are you doing right now?' he asked casually, like he hadn't just dropped off the face of the earth for the past fortnight.

'Erm, you've actually interrupted a really relaxing bath,' I said bluntly.

'I'm sorry it's been so long, I've been thinking about you a lot, Brooke.' He said softly, it's like I could hear his beautiful smile as he was talking to me, *what is wrong with you?* I thought to myself, but I stayed on the phone, hanging on to his every word like the idiot that I was, 'you've missed me a little bit too haven't you?' he stated confidently.

I smiled to myself, rubbing the smooth body wash up and down my tanned legs, 'I've been thinking about you a little bit too I guess' I admitted, ignoring his comment, he could pull the arrogance off.

'So why did you want me to come over again?' I asked, standing nervously at the front door. I knew it looked so desperate of me to turn up as soon as he rang, but there was no way I could spend another night drinking away my problems in a dingy club.

Liam's face lit up as he looked at me as intensely as always. I couldn't help but melt a little every time his big brown eyes looked my way.

'I've missed you!' he proclaimed loudly, gesturing for me to enter his home. I brushed up against him as I turned left into his living room, and the hairs all over my body stood on end. *Brooke, for god sake, pull yourself together* I thought to myself aggressively.

I entered a dark, plain room. There were two chocolate coloured sofas placed in an L shape in the middle, with a shabby wooden coffee table just in front of them. A large television hung on a grey wall and there was a table with some mismatch chairs scattered around it in the far corner, placed next to a small kitchen. There were photos of him and his mum everywhere.

'You ok?' he asked as he led me onto the biggest sofa with his hand placed gently on the middle of my back.

'Yeah, fine…' I muttered as I attempted to get comfortable, ignoring the rush that had surged through me from his touch.

'You're not though are you?' he frowned, slumping himself down next to me and reaching for a new box of cigarettes that were on the coffee table.

'Why wouldn't I be?' I smiled, trying to sound happy. I felt so nervous, I'd never allowed anyone to make me feel this way before and I wasn't best pleased that someone had broken down this barrier. I'd worked very hard to prevent that from happening.

'Because your mum has kicked you out and now you're spending your Friday night with a complete and utter idiot,' he stated bluntly as he blew the smoke away from my direction.

I raised my eyebrows, 'what makes you a complete and utter idiot?' I knew a few reasons; the fact that he'd turned me into a complete and utter wet lettuce being one of them.

'I haven't spoken to you for what? Two weeks?' he frowned at me again, his eyes locked onto mine.

I shrugged casually, attempting to act as though I hadn't checked my phone every single waking minute for the past 2 weeks and that the eye contact he was giving me was making it very difficult not to act on how I was feeling.

'You don't have to text me, I'm not really anything to you am I,' I replied as Liam's big, chocolate eyes continued to stare straight into mine, I looked down nervously, 'you always do that,'

'Do what?' he laughed, not breaking his eyes away from my face for one second.

'Stare into my soul, well I'm sorry but you'll find it's very black in there,' I kept the eye contact this time and realized why all those over times I looked away. If I stayed lost in them for too long then I knew I wouldn't make it back out alive. Liam chuckled before continuing his apology, I got the impression he had rehearsed this and I was ruining his flow, 'when I thought about it all and how whatever was going on with my mum and Guedo led to getting her killed, well I didn't want to involve you in something I thought you couldn't handle, but then I realized something…' he paused.

'And what was that?' I breathed.

'That who am I to decide what you can and cannot handle? I mean, I get the impression that you're pretty strong Brooke,'

'You do?' this made me smile from ear to ear.

'Yes, and I missed you just a little bit too,' he reassured me, squeezing my hand and smiling. I smiled back at him, I wanted to kiss him, I wanted to tell him how I felt, I wanted to rip his clothes off, but instead I dropped my gaze so he couldn't see my stupid smile.

'So yeah, do you accept my apology?' I nodded in reply and Liam squeezed my hand tighter, 'so for now, let me just say, without hope or agenda...'

'You are *not* about to finish that really nice apology off by quoting Love Actually to me are you Liam?' I interrupted.

'Wouldn't dream of it,' he smirked, 'I'm just a mechanic, standing in front of girl, asking her to forgive him,'

'Okay Julia Roberts, give it a rest,' I rolled my eyes.

'Erm, I'm defiantly Hugh Grant in that one,' he contended. 'So you think I'm strong? What gives you that impression?' I prodded, liking that I'd given off that impression. I'd been called a lot of names in my life, often by my mother-but never strong.

'I'm good at reading people,' he answered confidently.

'Oh, yeah?' I raised my eyebrows at him, 'can you read me?'

'You have a lot more going on in your life than people realize, and people don't realize because you're so good at hiding it. You go about day to day as if everything is fine, and you try and enjoy the little things that are good because you know that there is a lot of bad,' he paused and glanced at me for a second, 'and you're smart, talented, funny and...' he stopped.

And?' I prompted.

'Beautiful,' he whispered.

I blushed and gazed in adoration at him for a moment. How could someone who had known me for less than half a year already have a better understanding of me than anyone I had ever met in my life, Jamie included. I smiled timidly back at him.

'Well you're allowed to feel sorry for yourself and you're allowed to talk about it when you feel sad, Brooke. You're allowed.' He stated, squeezing my hand as he spoke. 'If you ever want to talk, I'm part of your life now so you can call me. I promise I won't disappear again.'

I smiled at his hand holding onto mine before swiftly changing the subject, 'what are these?' I glanced down at the coffee table to a pile of papers and picked them up.

He took them from me and rustled them up in his hands, 'I mean these people seem proper dangerous Brooke, the last two weeks it's all I've been reading, you don't have to get involved, I just wanted to show you what I found on mum's old computer,' he rambled, carefully searching through them until he came to what he was looking for, he handed it back to me.

'I'm in,' I reassured him as I studied the paper he had handed to me. It looked like a witness statement; I had seen a fair few of those recently at work.

Friday 2nd December, 1994.
15:32PM
I entered my office this morning, I clocked in at 8:17AM. 13 minutes before I was due to start. The door was ajar which I found strange as I always close it when I leave. As I opened the door my co-worker, Britney was laying on the floor in a pool of blood. I noticed a bullet wound to her head and some bruising to her face, there were clear signs of a struggle in my office.

'Then there's this,' Liam passed me a page which looked as though it had been ripped out of a diary, the page was dated the 2nd of December just like the witness statement.

There was some scribbled writing that I could just about make out, it read:
Just a reminder of how much I love you.
Meet me tomorrow at the place.
G xx

'Was that meeting the day she went missing, the Saturday?' I asked him, placing the papers back down onto the coffee table, he replied with a slow nod, 'oh...I don't know what to say, I'm so sorry.'

'I think that was aimed at my mum, reminding her that she couldn't get away from him?' I turned to him; his eyes were filled with tears.

'In some weird twisted way, maybe it was. Is this all you know?' I asked. Liam nodded in reply, 'well it's a lot of what if's, Liam. We need real evidence if we're going to find out what happened to your mum,'

He managed a smile, 'she would have loved you,'

'We will find out what happened to her,' I held his hand again. 'I promise you.'

He squeezed my hand tightly, 'what are the chances that you would work there, that we would even meet?' he smiled, 'at least something good has come out of this whole mess.' He used his free hand to tuck my hair behind my ears. 'Anyway, that's enough of this depressing talk for tonight!'

He pulled me up off of the sofa and guided me out of the room and up the creaky staircase, my heart pounded as we walked towards his bedroom, but I soon relaxed as he led me straight past it and into the room at the end of the hall.

As we walked through the door the smell of popcorn and scented candles hit me. The room was painted with a deep red and the carpeted floor was filled with beanbags. On the back wall hung a large projector screen and leant against the adjoining wall was an enormous bookshelf filled with countless DVD's, and of course a few videos scattered around the collection. Liam clutched my hand gently, beaming his magnificent grin.

'This is amazing, Liam,' I wondered at the towering bookshelf filled with every genre imaginable. I ran my fingers along the shelves directly in front of me, studying each title closely. *Gone With the Wind, An Affair to Remember, Roman Holiday, 10 Things I Hate About You, Casablanca, Dirty Dancing* and *The Notebook* were just a few of the many romantic films that Liam had raved about in our time spent together. All placed lovingly in a row.

'I'm assuming this is your go to shelf?' I giggled as I noticed how worn the cases were.

'Of course,' he smiled, 'but this…' he pulled out a DVD from the very end and held it proudly towards me, '…this is my favorite at the moment.'

'Let's put it on then,' I suggested. 'I've never seen When Harry Met Sally before,'

Liam's face dropped, 'you've never seen When Harry Met Sally? Oh you are so lucky I'm here to teach you about the world of cinema,' he joked. *I'm very lucky you are here Liam.* I thought, but I kept that to myself.

We curled up on a beanbag each and Liam wrapped a fluffy blanket over my shoulders. He dimmed the lights and the film begun.

Liam spoke over the infamous quotes of the film as if he had written the script himself, never missing a word or messing up a single line. *'Men and Women can't be friends because the sex part always gets in the way'* Harry and Liam spoke in unison, my heart rate tripled as he interlocked his fingers with mine.

We kept a hold of each other right up until the final sentence. Liam whispered, *'we were friends for a long time, and then we weren't and then we fell in love…'*

There was a moment of silence, with tension snaking through the air, before Liam spoke. 'So?' he grinned at me as the credits began to play, 'what did you think?'

'I love it,' I turned to him.

'Are you just saying that?' he frowned, I noticed he frowned a lot when he spoke, as if everything he said was said with force and meaning.

I laughed, 'No, No I promise, I loved it,' and I truly did. I had loved the whole evening and I didn't want it to end.

'Good,' he whispered.

'So does that mean I'm still welcome here? We can still be friends?' I joked as he twiddled my fingers around. His large hands made my fragile ones look as though they could break in his tight grip.
He was silent for a moment, as the credits stopped and the room darkened he looked at me so intensely that I felt as though everything around us had disappeared. He tucked a lose strand of hair delicately behind my ear and held it there for a second as he leaned forwards.

My heart fluttered as it had been doing most of the night. His hand slowly moved from my ear to my chest and then down to my waist, he forcefully pulled me in closer to him, our lips lingered millimeters away.

'What, no quote from Titanic? Ghost? Dirty Dancing?' I joked in almost a whisper.

Liam shook his head and smiled. I knew why. The moment was too perfect to disturb with anymore words. It seemed as though we had waited a long time to admit these feelings to ourselves and to each other. Thinking about it, I didn't mind the wait. He was the best thing I had ever waited for. At last our lips touched, our bodies intertwined, our clothes fell to the floor one by one. How could we resist? How I felt about him in that moment could start a fire and nobody could stand in a fire without being completely and utterly consumed by it.

I had 20 minutes left of work when I heard Mr. Daniels call my name. I walked into his room with a big, fake smile on my face. There was a lady already sitting at his desk.

'Would you be a star and show Miss Mcbeigh the way to reception please Brooke?' He always came across patronizing when he spoke, as if he believed that everyone else was rather inferior compared to him.

'Sure,' I replied, 'this way,' I gestured the dumpy, short lady to follow me. I pointed her in the right direction and then slowly headed back to the office. As I walked in he was sitting at his desk.

'Sir, do you have a minute?' I asked timidly.

'Of course, what can I help you with Brooke?' he switched his computer to standby and gestured for me to sit down.

Although our office was adjacent to his, we trainees never really had any dealings with him; he would leave us to be the problems of officers below him and as close as we would get to him was making his morning coffee. But I couldn't resist asking him about Britney Johnson.

'I have a friend who knew someone who used to work here. Her name was Georgina…' before I could finish the sentence I noticed Mr. Daniel's expression change immediately, *he remembers her*. 'You knew her?'

'Yes, I know who Georgina is,' He replied sternly, leaning back in his towering chair. 'Who's your friend?'

I was confused by his questioning, why did it matter who I was friends with?

'Erm, it's her son, Sir. I was just wondering what happened the day Britney was shot because that weekend his mum went missing,'

He looked at me for a few seconds before replying, as if he was thinking of the correct thing to say. 'I wasn't head of the department then; I hadn't been here for very long, this was what? 20 years ago?

'Yes, 25 years ago sir, it happened when my friend was 4,' I answered matter-of-factly.

He shook his head, 'well how am I supposed to remember something that happened 25 years ago Brooke,' he looked bewildered, as If he was a deer in headlights.

I frowned at him, 'sorry sir, I just wanted to know, I'm sure you can understand he just wants to find out about his mum?'

'Aren't you a little young to be hanging around with a 28 year old anyway Brooke?' he asked.

I was becoming angered with his rude questioning, I'd never been around him alone for long enough to realise what an unpleasant man he was. 'I'm 24, sir, not really,' I replied bluntly.

He stood up and walked towards the window. 'That bench over there, night after night you sit there with that rugged boy,'

I was thrown by this comment, 'Yeah, that's my friend?'

'I don't want my employees to be seen having friends like *that*,' he remarked.

His comment reminded me of how snobby my mother could be and this instantly put me in defense mode. 'I'm guessing you speak to him about topics from work then, if he is asking about his mum and Britney,'

I folded my arms and glared at him crossly, 'Well no actually, because most of what I know is about an ongoing investigation so I couldn't talk about them even if I wanted to.'

He sneered at me and walked back to his desk, standing over me as if he was attempting to be intimidating, 'don't give me that bull, Brooke.'

'It's not sir, it's the truth,' I looked up at him, making eye contact to show him that he doesn't scare me in the slightest, 'I really want to pass my apprenticeship and do this job, and If I was walking around talking about classified information to random people then I wouldn't have much of a chance would I?'

'He's probably just using you for information, you're young and vulnerable, he will drop you as soon as he realises you don't know anything.' He sneered at me.

I was astounded at how this conversation had panned out, I couldn't believe I had been working for such an arrogant man and not even realized it. 'Don't know anything about what sir?' I stood up, attempting to act as confident as I possibly could in that moment.

He leaned in close to me, his breath reeked of coffee and tobacco, 'sometimes, Brooke, people are too clever for their own good and they dig a little too deeply, and these people need to learn that they are playing a very dangerous game.' 'Are you threatening me, sir?' I glared at him.

'Of course not, Brooke,' he smiled.

'Sir, do you know who Guedo Altair is?' I studied his face looking for a reaction-and I definitely got one. His eyes grew large and his face turned crimson.

'It's the end of the day, Brooke,' he replied sternly, 'I suggest you leave, and maybe rethink who you are befriending before somebody ends up getting hurt.'

With that I retrieved my bag from the office and left. I'd taken that as a yes he 100 percent did know who Guedo was. I kept walking. I didn't stop for Liam at the bench; I just rushed straight past and kept on running down the road to where my car was parked. I could hear the thump of Liam's footsteps chasing after me, but I carried on hurrying away until I reached the under path. I leant against the graffiti covered wall and let out a sigh of relief.

'Brooke!' Liam's voice vibrated through the tunnel, 'where are you going?'

'Of course the fucking car park was full this morning, when I want to drive away fast,' I panted as Liam caught up with me,

'I don't think we should do this anymore,' I sighed as he held onto my shoulders.

'Do what?' he questioned, a wave of disappointment crashed across his face.

'I want to help you find out what happened to your mum, but he knows who you are. I can't let you get hurt,' I spluttered out, tears rolling down my frost bitten cheeks.

'Who is gonna hurt me?' he asked, his eyes scanning our surroundings frantically.

'Mr. Daniels, I think he knows something,' I whispered. Liam didn't say anything, he just pulled me towards his warm body and wrapped his arms around me; I was still shaking.

'B, are you okay?' Jamie frowned as Liam and I rushed into the warm living room.

I knew she would gather that something was wrong soon or later-she could read me like a book. I nodded. I could feel a lump in my throat and I knew if I spoke I would just begin to cry again.

'Don't lie to me, what's going on?' she insisted as she sat up in the chair.

'She's fine she just had a long day at…' Liam tried to save me, but Jamie wasn't having that.

'…I wasn't asking you, Liam. I was asking *her*,' Jamie snapped loudly.

'It's just my boss, he said some things to me today and it scared me that's all,' I croaked.

Jamie immediately got up and sat beside me, 'well he clearly done a lot more than just scare you, you never get scared by anything people say so he obviously said something bad,' she put her arm around me, 'he can't do this to you, it must be under some employees rights that he has to treat you with respect, right?'

I shrugged my shoulders and switched on the TV, not wanting to appear frightened in front of either of them. 'All I'm saying is the name Daniel is bad luck,' I joked in an attempt to lessen her worry.

Jamie smiled, 'I hear you there sister,' Liam looked at both of us with a confused expression on his face, 'long story,' Jamie nodded at him, 'your middle name isn't Daniel is it?'

My surroundings were dark and misty; the owl's calls echoed through the gaps between the trees and the stars glistened brightly. The light of the moon was reflecting magically as if the trees were made from pure glass. My heart was drumming loudly against my chest. A rush of cold wind blew past me, blowing my long, hair with it.

A chill travelled down my spine as if someone had just walked over my grave. Then I realised someone did, I did. I looked down and there I was, my name carved into a grey, marble slab.

A twig cracked behind me and I turned around to see Mr. Daniels towering over me. I tried to run, but I fell backwards onto the grave, mud started to seep over my legs.

I noticed that there were figures slowly walking towards me as I sank lower. The figures had blurred faces, but I could see that it was my mum, dad and the twins, Jamie, Liam and Mr. Daniels all looking down at me. A voice in my head was saying *hold out you hand*. I reached out and Liam grabbed me, as he pulled me up, everyone else disappeared.

It was just Liam and I; standing in the middle of the moon lit forest...'Brooke...' Liam started to speak in the most magical voice. But slowly his face begun to melt away, his voice became deep and gruff and drowned out by my bloodcurdling screams.

I sat up in a cold sweat; it had been a long time since I'd had a nightmare that bad-but it didn't compare in the slightest to the sleep paralysis and night terrors I'd suffered from as a child.

Thankful that I could sit up, I looked around the room. Jamie was sprawled out next to me in her bed, fast asleep. Liam was on the floor; his head was resting up against Jamie's beanbag. His brown curly hair was veering off in all directions, his nose flared slightly as he breathed in and out.

Even though there was enough bedrooms in this house for us all to sleep in, they had both insisted on staying in the same room as me.

I sat there for several minutes, thinking about nothing but my confusing conversation with Mr. Daniels. 'Brooke?' I heard a whisper from the floor. I looked down at Liam's sleepy eyes gazing up at me, 'you okay?'

I slid off of the bed-being careful not to wake Jamie up-and sat next to him, 'yes,' I whispered back, 'I just had a bad dream.'

'I've been thinking,' Liam said, scooting to the left so I could get under the covers.

'Did it hurt?' I giggled childishly, thinking back to all of the times my dad had aimed that joke at my mum and how it never received a laugh.

He nudged me, 'shut up. Look I don't want this affecting your job. So I'll just carry on without you.'

'No you won't,' I snapped at him, Jamie stirred in her sleep so I gestured for him to follow me downstairs.

'Brooke, I can't just sit around and do nothing,' he argued as we snuck down the stairs.

'I know, but you're not doing it alone!' I pulled him onto the sofa and chucked a blanket over us.

He grabbed my hands and looked me straight in the eye, 'look at how scared you were though. It's gonna be more of that,'

'He just surprised me, I wasn't expecting all of that yesterday,' I reassured him.

Of course this wasn't the truth, the anxiety inside of me had been bubbling away in my stomach since Mr. Daniels and I had our run in. I knew it was only a matter of time before the emotions came falling out of me, it always happened one way or another. *I really need to go back to counseling.* I made a mental note; I couldn't keep avoiding it forever.

He squeezed my hands tighter, 'we will have to be smarter about this then. No more meeting on that bench so he can see us; we need to make it look like we don't see each other anymore. We'll talk about the rest in the morning; I don't even know what's going on.' Liam sighed, sliding his head down so it was resting on the arm of the chair and pulling me onto his chest. He kissed my forehead, 'get some sleep girl.'

I woke up the next morning with Liam's arm still wrapped around me. The bright light from the window lit up the room. I looked up at Liam, still sleeping. His warm breath was blowing against my face. I giggled as it tickled me, he stirred and woke up.

'Sorry,' I laughed, 'I didn't mean to wake you up.'

'What's so funny?' he asked grumpily, rubbing his eyes with his free hand and squinting in the light. I grinned up at him.

'What?' he smiled back at me.

Before I could answer, Jamie swung open the door and starred at us suspiciously, 'morning lovebirds,'

'Morning,' I replied as I jumped up from my place on Liam's chest, feeling like a teenager hiding her boyfriend from her parents.

'B, come here,' she ordered as she waltzed into the kitchen, 'so, what's the story with him then?' she hissed as she turned the kettle on.

I ignored her, retrieving some tea cups out of the cupboard as slowly as I could.

Jamie grabbed my shoulder and turned me around, 'I am your best friend, we tell each other everything and we have done for 17 years. So you are going to tell me what's going on with you and Mr. Big eyes curly hair over there?'

I laughed, 'Jamie, if there was anything going on I would tell you, but there isn't...'

Jamie rolled her eyes dramatically, 'of course something has happened!' I didn't reply, but my face must have given the answer away as I thought back to the other night. 'Oh my god!' she screeched.

'Shh!' I hissed at her, laughing, 'yes, maybe something happened, but only once, it doesn't mean anything!'

'Aw, It's about time you got a boyfriend, I was sick of getting all of the boys,' I raised my eyebrows at her, 'okay, I wasn't at all. But he is SO much better than big mouth Daniel,' she said as she carried on making tea.

'His not my boyfriend anyway, I guess we're not really anything, but yeah I do really like him...' I blushed. I'd had enough of being interrogated for one morning and walked back into the front room. I noticed that Liam was smirking at me with an amused look on his face.

'What?' I said, sitting back down next to him.

'Nothing,' he replied as he put the cover over us again, 'you and Jamie want to come round mine today? I was thinking of having a few mates over for a party, thought I should introduce you to them all sooner or later right?'

'Sounds good,' I smiled.

'Did I just hear the word party?' Jamie popped her head into the room, 'take it I'm invited to this?'

'Yeah, course Jamie,' Liam shouted back, 'can hear things from the kitchen you know,' he grinned at me. I realized what that smug look on his face was for now, my cheeks flushed red and I looked away.

The last time my life was 'normal'
'I think you should acknowledge your accomplishments a bit more, don't you?' Dr. Daw asked softly, as I'd explained briefly the tedious, repetitive nonsense that was my life.

I'd been counselling since I was about 9 years old and it had become part of my routine now. I'd had periods of a year or so where I wouldn't need to go, but then the anxiety would creep up on me again-like it had recently-and my mum would insist on me re-visiting Dr. Daw, probably because it was easier to pay for me to speak to a stranger than sit and listen to her own daughter herself. Of course now it was different, I had to pay Dr. Daw myself.

'My accomplishments?' I queried, 'none spring to mind,'

'If you had to name one accomplishment from your whole life, what would it be?' she leant forwards in her chair.

Today she was wearing a very expensive looking Chanel necklace and matching earring set. Her hair, as always, was scooped up in a perfectly placed diamante clip on top of her head.

I'd always wondered if Dr. Daw ever let lose, I knew her name was Roxanne and ever since watching the film Moulin Rouge when I was younger I couldn't get it out of my head that Dr. Daw was actually a prostitute on the red light district, and you know, she'd just got a degree in counselling as something on the side. But there I was again, making unreal scenarios up in my head so that I didn't have to face reality- this is something she had told me I had a habit of doing.

'Probably my job,' I replied after a while of mulling over possible accomplishments I could think of. There weren't many at all.

'Okay, yes your job is a huge accomplishment, all those years of university with your crippling anxiety, you got through it and now you're training in a field you love,'

Love is a strong word. I thought, but I nodded and smiled in agreement.

'What about your relationships? You've managed to keep the same best friend for your whole life, that's admirable. And you waited to get a boyfriend that truly values who you are, you didn't settle for anything less than you deserve.' She complimented, which made me quite uncomfortable. *I wondered if anyone had the answer to what you were supposed to do and where you were supposed to look when someone paid you a compliment.*

'I don't have a boyfriend, Liam isn't my boyfriend,' I insisted.

'Okay, you have a special friend then,' she corrected herself.

Special friend? What is this woman going on about? I bit my lip so I wouldn't laugh.
'And I think the biggest accomplishment of all is that you haven't been having panic attacks for a while.'

That much was true for now, but with everything going on I didn't know how long it would last. I had always suffered with incapacitating panic attacks, bought on by my anxiety disorder. I had been diagnosed by many doctors, paediatricians and therapists at the age of 7 as I would often end up in hospital as a result of not being able to breathe. We ruled out asthma, lung cancer (which my mum was adamant I had, ever the drama queen) and all other physical illnesses until I had seen a child therapist who professionally diagnosed me as having anxiety with just a hint of depression, you know just something a little extra for some added flare.

I wasn't one to talk about it, or let people know that I had a weakness-so coming to counselling was a nice escape for me. I liked Dr. Daw too, she said some stupid things sometimes that only someone with a degree would say, but she was nice enough.

'What I am trying to say is you should be more aware of the many accomplishments you have made for a girl still in her early twenties, Brooke. I know you have expressed before that you feel as though your family are not proud of you, or that Jamie doesn't really understand the significance of your job, but you can still be proud of yourself. At the end of the day, isn't that the only opinion that matters?'

As I walked out of the waiting room, feeling like I could hold my head a little higher, I heard Daniel's voice call out after me. 'Sorry, can't stop, I have a thing,' I shouted back as I rushed out of the door. Maybe I shouldn't hold my head too high, I thought. I was still treating Daniel like he didn't exist anymore.

'Do you want me to do your hair?' I asked Jamie as we sat in the compact and bare spare room of Liam's house.

I began to brush through her long, soft hair, 'I miss being little Brooke, my mum used to brush my hair for me every morning like this, why did all of that change?'

'I thought you liked being alone?' I asked as I wrapped her soft hair around some curling tongs.

'No, I mean it's alright, but it gets boring,' she replied, 'don't you miss your parents and the twins?'

I was silent. I had spoken to the twins on the phone when they were with Auntie Ron, but I hadn't heard a word from either of my parents, 'I miss Riley and Ruby, but they seem like they are okay without me,' I replied after a while.

'Do you think our parents even miss us?' her voice cracked a little. It wasn't like her to become emotional over her parents, I wondered if they'd recently had a falling out.

'Probably not, they've always been selfish. That's why I'm glad I have had you all these years. We would be so lonely otherwise.' I attempted to cheer her up.

'Hmm…' she sighed.

'I like it, being independent. I've grown up with my mum telling me how to act, dress and speak and I couldn't step out of line, ever.'
'I know, I've noticed you're a lot more fun without her around,' she managed a weak laugh, 'I got a text earlier saying that mum and dad will be back for a day and then they are going up to visit my mum's cousins in Devon, but no invite for me,'

'It's messed up, you work so hard to look after yourself. I'm sorry babe. The last time I heard from my mum she text me telling me it was better without me there, so yeah that's that,'

'It's fine, you know what though B, I think we should find a place of our own-together, we're adults now, we should probably stop pining after our childhood.'

'How much fun would that be?' I smiled, 'promise?'

'I promise, we'll start looking as soon as possible, but what about Liam?' she wondered, as she touched up her makeup in the small compact mirror she had in her bag.

'What about him?' I frowned.

'Won't you be spending more time with him now that you're all loved up,' she glanced at me in the reflection as I blushed at the thought of him.

'We're defiantly not loved up, we're not even together, and even if we were, you'll always come first,' I insisted.

'I like him for you,' she said coolly.

'Yeah, he'll do,' I laughed, finishing off her hair and sitting on the floor next to her.

'Just don't ditch me for him; boys aren't everything you know,' she added.

'Coming from *you*,' I laughed.

It's always just been me and you,' she ignored my joke, obviously not up for any arguments today. I thought I'd best appreciate this rare occasion.

'And it's always will be, nothing is going to change now that we're getting older.' I assured her.

She sighed as he hugged me. I felt a tear creep into my eyes, I was so lucky that I had such a close friend, I felt so guilty for not telling her about everything that was going on in my life, I had always told her everything. But Liam's business wasn't mine to tell, so for now I'd have to keep it quiet.

After about an hour and a half of Jamie and I getting ready and talking, there was a knock at Liam's door. I listened as the door creaked open; there were some faint mutters from the other side.

I heard a deep voice say, 'How you been man?'

And another slightly higher voice say, 'yeah bro, been a while.'

We sat in the room silently, listening into their conversation. I heard Liam say, 'how's your bird, Billy?'

The one with the deeper voice answered for him, 'probably sexually frustrated,' there were roars of laughter from this apparently funny comment.
The boy that I assumed was Billy butted in, the only one not laughing. 'Leave it out,' he said, his wimpy voice could hardly be heard over the booming laughter.

'Just a joke, bruv,' said the boy who had made the comment, 'chill,'

'Girls!' Liam shouted up the stairs, 'you ready?'

'Girls?' all of the boys said in unison.

We looked at each other and laughed at their typical male behavior. Jamie flicked her hair and shouted back, 'yeah!'

We slowly walked downstairs, careful not to fall over in our ridiculously high heels. 'Who wears heels like this to a house party Jamie, I feel like an idiot,' I hissed at her.

'Brooke, take it from me, the expert, we defiantly do not look like idiots,' she reassured me, flicking her hair over her shoulder for the millionth time in 5 minutes.

As we entered the front room, everyone stopped what they were doing and stared, the room was filled with silence for a few seconds.

I smiled at everyone and held Jamie's arm. 'Hi,' I greeted them politely.

'Why is everyone so gormless?' Jamie whispered into my ear.

'Aren't you used to things with dicks staring at you?' I whispered back, leading her into the kitchen to get some drinks.
I peered over at Liam; he was sitting on the sofa next to a skinny, blonde boy who seemed to be suffering with severe acne problems. His teeth stuck out so he couldn't even close his mouth and he was dressed differently from the rest of the boys. The others were all clad head to toe in designer clothes whereas this one was wearing a *CSI* jumper and some old, warn out jeans.

They seemed to be lost in a deep conversation. Liam was frowning, as always. Walking back into the room with our glasses filled to the brim we stood by Liam and the *CSI* boy. I smiled at him and he smiled back, showing off his ridiculously goofy teeth even more, 'I'm Brooke, this is Jamie,' I said.

'Hello, I am Billy. It's very nice to meet you both,' he replied in a very posh, stereo typical English accent. *My mum would love you* I thought.

A big, bulky boy walked over and stood in front of us, 'Alright,' he nodded, I remembered his face from the first night I'd met Liam, 'nice to see ya again, Brooke,'

'Hi, it's Dale, right?' I smiled at him as he nodded, 'this is my friend Jamie,'

'Beautiful name,' he winked as he said this, 'my dog was called Jamie, she died,'

'Oh, I'm sorry,' I bit my lip to hold back the laughter. I felt Jamie dig her nails into my arm as she let out a squeak.

'Jamie and Brooke,' Dale repeated, 'nice,' he grinned as he slid past us and into the kitchen where he started an annoyingly loud conversation with a big group of boys who were all in deep discussions over bottles of beer and cigarettes.

 Jamie being Jamie had already sniffed out the men she found attractive and strutted into the kitchen to flirt outrageously with everyone in the room as usual. I laughed and sat down next to Liam, moving my focus to their conversation.

'So what can you do?' Liam was asking Billy.

'I can hack into computers, phones-pretty much anything you want me to,' Billy replied, nervously looking my way, 'is she meant to hear this, isn't she police?'

I answered on Liam's behalf, 'I'm not police, and if it's for Liam you could murder someone in front of me and I wouldn't care,'

Billy eased up a bit as I spoke, 'she's been helping,' Liam explained.

'Well I won't be murdering anyone in front of you Brooke, but I can help in any way I can, I work as a criminal profiler, I have a degree in computing, I'm perfect for the job' Billy answered confidently.

'That's amazing,' I exclaimed, kissing Liam on the cheek, 'is there anything we can do to help you?'

'I'm sure there will be, I'm only a geek-I wouldn't be able to fight anyone. Our kind isn't really famous for that,' he joked. My stomach flipped as Billy mentioned fighting. I had tried to avoid thinking about how deep we were getting into this. Mr. Daniels' voice echoed through my head *'and they dig a little too deeply, and these people need to learn that they are playing a very dangerous game.'* I shuddered and changed the subject quickly.

After a while, more and more people began to pile into Liam's small home, it made me happy knowing that although Liam hadn't experienced the best start to life he clearly had so many people around him that cared about him.

It was around 1am and I had made my way outside, allowing myself a break from the growing crowd of people and loud music. I slumped myself down on the step that led into the garden room and shivered as I chugged on a cigarette and sipped what must have been my 10th glass of wine. The skimpy dress I was wearing was not fit for being outside in the winter, but I had swapped my uncomfortable heels for a pair of slippers I had packed so at least I'd still have my toes in the morning.

I watched through the glass door at everyone laughing and dancing. I held my head up to the sky and smiled as the stars sparkled brightly into my eyes.

The door creaked open and I looked down to see Liam walking towards me, 'beautiful aren't they, the stars?' I slurred.

He laughed as he sat down next to me on the cold step, 'yeah, beautiful...,' he agreed as he watched me laugh hysterically at myself for no apparent reason.
After I had lost the giggles, I turned to him and stared seriously, 'thank you for being there for me, Liam. With my mum kicking me out and everything, you have been such a good friend, I'm so glad I met you,' he looked down to the floor as I said this, sighing. 'What's wrong?' I held his hand and squeezed it, 'Billy is going to help us, everything is going to be fine,' I grinned at him.

'I know I know...' he said as he looked into my eyes once again.

'Well, what then?' I frowned.

'I heard you and Jamie talking in the kitchen at hers earlier…' he began.

'…I know you did, you basically told me that,' I interrupted, 'did you not want me to say anything to her?'

He pulled the hand that I was holding up to my cold, windswept face and cupped my cheek, 'she's your best friend, why would I want you to keep anything from her?' he studied my face closely.

I shrugged and tilted my face into his warm hand a little bit more, 'I don't know, maybe you'd want to keep me a secret?'

'I'd want the world to know,' he smiled. My heart skipped a beat as he continued to speak, 'I don't just see you as a friend, Brooke…' he whispered.

'Neither do I, so, what do you want to…' but before I could finish my sentence, Liam pulled me close and interrupted me with a kiss.
I'd been yearning for us to share a kiss since the other night; I couldn't stop thinking about how one kiss from him sent my body into overdrive, 'I want you,' I whispered drunkenly.

'Now?' he grinned, throwing a look at everyone through the glass before pulling me to an upright position and pushing open the door that we were sitting by. We fell into the darkness; Liam fumbled around for the light switch which dimly lit up the conservatory style room, he turned the key to lock the door and looked fiercely at me, 'can I just say you look out of this world tonight girl.' He complimented, placing his big hands around my waist which was perfectly outlined in my tight mini dress.

'Yes, you can just say,' I giggled as I pushed him backwards onto the velvet tub chair that was placed in the corner of the room and perched myself onto his lap.

Liam smiled dotingly up at me, 'I haven't stopped thinking about you, not for one second,' he confessed. His big, brown eyes seemed to light up as he spoke.

'Me either,' I agreed, swishing my hair so it fell behind my shoulders.

'You should be kissed and often, and by someone who knows how,' he breathed.

'Gone with the Wind?' I chuckled.

'You're getting good at this, girl. ' he replied in a whisper before kissing me again, sending me to a whole other world.

I sat up and looked around me; I was lying on the garden room floor wrapped in a blanket, I peered through the glass into the main house. Most people had left, but Dale and two of his friends-whose names I had learned were Chris and Nathan-were still there, lying on the kitchen floor, hugging bottles of beer.

 I heard some voices in the garden and turned around to see Liam and Jamie sitting on the bench at the back, having a cigarette and a cup of tea. I wrapped myself in the blanket and joined them outside.

'How do you two manage to drink so much, but manage to look fine in the morning?' Liam questioned us as I sat on Jamie's lap, squinting in the morning sun.

'Oh why thank you Liam,' Jamie replied, 'are you naked under their B?' she laughed.

'I don't know,' I said, but the voice that came out sounded like I had been possessed by a demon, they both burst out laughing.

'Alright Bob,' Jamie snorted; 'where did you two disappear to last night anyway, did you sleep in there?' she nodded towards the garden room.

Liam was gazing at me fondly; I blushed as I remembered the events of the night before, 'yeah, Brooke was very drunk so I thought I'd best take her somewhere quieter,' Liam answered with a smirk on his face.

'Oh take her somewhere quieter,' Jamie repeated with a sarcastic tone, 'can't you keep it in your pants for one night, fancy the host of the party leaving everyone!'
Liam laughed, 'you weren't complaining, you had everyone eating out of the palm of your hand last night, miss.'

I smiled as I listened to my best friend, and who I guessed was now my boyfriend, joking around with each other. Why couldn't life always have been this good?

For the days that followed Billy, Liam and I used any spare time we had to catch up with each other about Liam's mum. Liam had decided to tell Jamie as she was asking me questions whenever I walked through the door, she said she was willing to help, but usually just made us drinks and nodded in agreement at anything we said.

Work had been extra busy too; the department were working day and night on finding out whom 'seven' was. Andrew Spence had been no help at all and the mood at work was very tense-especially where Mr. Daniels was concerned.

He hadn't mentioned another word of Liam and I, so I believed he had noticed that I wasn't meeting him outside work, or texting him throughout the duration of the day.

'I think I've found something,' Billy said excitedly. We were all in our usual spots in Jamie's living room, with laptops, tablets and beer bottles scattered everywhere. 'The girl you worked with Harriet, the one who has gone missing. I've found where her boyfriend lives, we could stop by and see if she is there?'

I turned to Billy, utterly confused, 'when did this-what-what?' Liam looked just as confused as me, which I was glad to see. Billy stared at me for a moment, wondering if I was going to finish that sentence or not, 'Well, I just thought it was weird that Mr. D threatened you…' Billy began, but before he could finish his sentence Jamie shot up from her seat.

'He *threatened* you?' she screeched, 'was this when you came home that day all shaken up? I knew there was something wrong!'

'Jamie, calm down,' I rolled my eyes at her, she had been prone to a lot more outbursts than usual as of late.

'Calm down? *Calm down*? How can I fucking calm down when *he* has got you into this mess?' she shouted at me, pointing towards Liam who was sitting dumbfounded next to me, he always looked in complete shock at Jamie's sudden explosions of anger.

I stood up and stormed over to her, 'don't you dare bring Liam into this. It's not his fault that my boss is a prick!'

'Oh that's it,' she laughed, 'protect your precious boyfriend, well do you know what, I liked you a lot better when you were the sad pathetic virgin who didn't think she was flipping inspector gadget or something,' Liam sniggered from behind me, Billy glanced down to the floor tapping his toes nervously together.

'At least I can get a boyfriend, anyone of the million skanks you've slept with called you back yet?' I replied harshly, I knew I'd taken it too far then, 'Jamie…' I sighed as she slammed the living room door in my face and ran upstairs, 'oh for fuck sake,' I exhaled.

Liam looked at me, 'that was…'
'Yes I know, that was a bitch thing to say to my best friend, she'll be fine, onto more important things,' I snapped, slumping back onto the sofa, 'go on Billy, you were saying about Mr. Daniels threatening me?'

A bedroom door slammed upstairs and what sounded like one of her very expensive mirrored lamps went crashing against a wall, but Billy being the professional he was carried on speaking as though there wasn't a 24 year old girl having a mental breakdown in her bedroom upstairs.

'Well the fact that Mr. Daniels threatened you, and then Harriet…' CRASH, another piece of expensive décor went hurdling against a wall. '…then Harriet didn't come back to work after you seeing her with a dodgy looking guy, which you said…'

'AAAAAARRRRGGGHHHHHH' Jamie's squeal echoed down the stairs.

'...which you said,' Billy spoke louder, 'was out of character for her,'

'You're doing well, Bill,' Liam chortled, I shot him a disapproving look, but couldn't keep a straight face for long, I couldn't function as a normal human being whenever he smiled.

'It couldn't hurt just seeing what happened to her, if all else fails, you've found out what came of your friend so it's a win, win really isn't it?' Billy stated.
'So we go there, see what's going on with her, if she knows anything about Mr. D...' I stopped in my tracks. I knew when Dr. Daniels had reacted to my questions about Guedo and Georgina in the way he did that there was something not right, that maybe somehow he was involved. But Billy's clever mind linking Harriet, Mr. Daniels, my work and Liam's mum all together had suddenly put everything in to perspective for me.

Another bang shook the ceiling, breaking my silence, 'Billy, show me Georgina's emails again.'

Billy slid across the sofa to sit next to me and bought up her email account. There it was, as clear as day in front of us. Her inbox was filled with newspaper articles, links and research she had emailed herself from her work account, all with one subject-Human Trafficking. How could I have been so naïve to what was there right in front of me, in my job of all places?

Mr. Daniels' threat really was something I should have taken seriously. Mr. Daniels was the head of my department, a department who had been investigating a series of organised crime related to human trafficking long before I had arrived there. He was working there when Liam's mum went missing, and when Brittany was killed. I realised that there had been no real breakthroughs in the case, especially in the years that he had been acting lead, just enough to not cause suspicion or investigation. My head felt as though it was about to explode with endless possibilities. Was I going mad, or could it be that the place I wanted to work at so badly was lead by a very corrupt man?

'Brooke?' Liam's voice broke my trail of thoughts, 'what is it?' I looked at his mesmerizingly stunning face, full of hope and pain all at the same time. I didn't want to burden him with the thought of his mum being involved in a trafficking circle, I didn't want to reveal what I knew to everyone, and I needed to process it first.

'Nothing, I just don't like arguing with Jamie,' I lied, 'sorry Billy, I didn't mean to go off topic, and it sounds like a great idea. Do you think Harriet is going to be there? We'll need to get inside.'

Jamie walked back into the room, mascara smudged around her eyes, she seemed to have calmed down.

'She, she does have a point there,' Billy nervously replied, his eyes followed Jamie anxiously as he spoke, 'we need to get in the house if we are going to find anything, otherwise it will be a waste of time'

'Well that's what breaking and entering is for,' Jamie snapped sarcastically as she slumped back down on the armchair.

'Do you want to leave it until tomorrow, Brooke?' Liam asked, ignoring Jamie's outburst completely, 'have a think about it?'

'Do you?' I stood up, looking down at him, he shook his head, 'well then, what are we waiting for?' come on let's go,' I requested.

Billy, Liam and I piled into Billy's car, leaving Jamie sulking at the house. Liam constantly lent back from the passenger's seat to squeeze my leg or ask if I was ok. But the look in his eyes showed excitement, I couldn't stop thinking about the night we were going to have once this day was over and all of the adrenaline would be rushing through us still.

We drove past the address slowly, there didn't seem to be anyone there. Billy circled around the area again and parked a few houses up. I immediately ran to the chipped front door and knocked a few times, 'Brooke,' I heard Billy hiss from behind me, 'what the *fuck* are you doing,'

'She's alright, she's got this,' Liam smirked at me, his eyes filled with desire.

'No one is answering!' I called over to them, disappointed. I was hoping that Harriet would welcome me in with open arms and tell me everything I needed to know. I wanted to be the one to bring good news to Liam.

'What do we do now?' Billy whispered as we all crouched under a window in the side alley. Liam shrugged, scanning the area. I rolled my eyes as I looked around for a way in. The alley way was narrow; there was a rusty gate at the other end which looked as though it was leading into a garden.

I peered above me and noticed that the window we were under was slightly open, 'Liam, go look into the garden…' I instructed under my breath, 'I'm gonna try get in here,' I said as I gently pushed open the window.

'Are you mad?' Billy panicked.

'Yeah, she is,' Liam smirked earnestly again at me before sneaking over to the fence.

I looked into the open window; there was a small, somber room on the other side. I could faintly make out a bed and a chest of drawers, 'Billy,' I hissed, 'help me up,'

'I really don't think this…' he stammered.

'…you only have to help me up, you don't have to do anything else,' I said as he pushed me up towards the window which was just a few inches taller than me.

'You want me to just stand out here on my own?' he complained.

I managed to get one of my legs into the room, I looked back at him, 'come in with me then, just make a decision now please,'

'Okay, okay. I'm coming,' he respired.

I swung my other leg over the window and jumped down into the room. Billy followed shortly after me, 'what about Liam?'

'Liam can look after himself,' I replied half heartedly as I began to look around the room. I opened the drawers and rifled through them, but there was nothing-just men's underwear, socks and packs of cigarettes.

I turned around to Billy looking under the busted bed, 'found anything?' I whispered. He emerged back out and shook his head. 'Guess we're gonna have to go out there,' I sighed. I put my ear against the bedroom door, but I couldn't hear any movement. I gestured for Billy to come with me.
I crept around the half open door; eager to get inside. All of the curtains were drawn and none of the light switches were working, I pulled out my phone from my bag and shone the light around the room to get a better look. There was a tatty sofa by the window, a table was placed in the middle with some chairs around it; there were some empty beer bottles and stubbed out cigarette butts in an astray placed on the table and scatters of Tobacco all over the floor.

Billy brushed past me and walked around the table to the back wall of the room where there was a pin board, 'this doesn't look like somewhere Harriet would live,' I frowned. I tip toed next to him and watched as his eyes lit up over every photo that was pinned on there. 'What?' I asked facing my phone light towards him.

'Look at this,' he murmured, pointing to a photo at the very bottom. It was a photo of a man and woman dressed smartly, they were both smiling and they had their hands up in a waving position. The lady had a red circle around her with an arrow coming off of it; at the end of the arrow was some writing:

Rebecca Stevens-Prison

Rebecca's photo was part of a row of photographs all labelled with the same bright red marker pen. There were a few women that I didn't recognize, all with red crosses over their faces; I noticed Britney Johnson-she too had a red cross covering her face. I knew then what that meant for all of those women, I shivered.

'There's no Georgina on this wall,' I acknowledged, 'I'm guessing that's a good thing seeing as this Rebecca woman is in prison and Britney's dead,'
Billy pulled out his phone and took a few photos of the board, before turning his attention elsewhere around the room, 'It really smells like weed in here,' he stated as he inspected the cramped living room some more.

I nodded as I rustled through some books and notepads that were sprawled across the sofa. I recognised Harriet's neat handwriting.

'Billy, listen to this,' I called out to him as he began investigating the kitchen area. 'Matt was told by some work mates today that seven, the person in charge, was moving abroad in July. That's what Harriet has written in this diary. Seven is the person we've been investigating at work.'

'Has she dated it?' Billy called back.

'This is the last entry, it was written almost 2 weeks ago.' I answered, flicking through the other pages of the notepad. I passed Billy through the kitchen area and into the back garden to see what Liam was doing, I scanned the whole garden looking for him, but he was nowhere to be seen. I noticed a wooden dog house in the far corner.

I held up my hand as Billy ran out after me, 'shh,' I snapped.

'Liam,' I whispered across the garden, there was no answer, 'fuck…' I exclaimed, holding my head in my hands.

'Well I don't think the dog has eaten him or anything,' Billy muttered into my ear, nodding towards the dog house. I stared at him dumbfounded by how someone so clever could come out with such a stupid comment, 'okay, that was stupid,' he said as he saw my reaction, 'what do we do now?' I ignored him, walking over to the dog house. I knelt down and looked inside, 'fuck!' I screamed as something jumped out at me. I looked up and let out a sigh of relief as I saw Liam's head of curly hair leaning over me, 'what the hell are you doing?' I yelled at him.

Liam seemed to be very amused by how scared I was, 'I'm sorry, I heard a noise and hid in here, I didn't know it was you. I take it the dog isn't in there?'

I shook my head as he helped me up, I was about to show Liam the notebook when the sound of a car pulling up on the drive stopped me. Without thinking I ran towards the fence, but a tall figure began to speed up the alley way towards me. The mystery dog barked loudly from the back of the car.

'Oi, who the fuck are you?' they shouted. I recognised his voice.

Liam and Billy were standing by the back door, waving for me to follow them, we ran frantically back into the kitchen. Just as we reached the living room, the front door opened, the person strolled confidently through it.

Liam and Billy jumped behind the sofa before he could see them, but I wasn't as quick, 'I ain't gonna ask you again, who the fuck are you?'

I froze on the spot, 'Matt?' I questioned apprehensively, *you can turn this around Brooke.* I said to myself.

'How do you know my name?' he demanded as he walked towards me.

I took a few steps backwards every time he drew closer, 'you're Harriet's boyfriend right? We met at the Christmas fair remember?' I reminded him. He looked even worse than I remembered. His eyes were sunken and tired and his skin looked grey and weathered.

'And what the fuck are you doing in my house?' he asked, pulling something from the back of his frayed jeans.

'Brooke?' Harriet's voice followed through the front door. She was holding onto the snarling dogs lead tightly, her eyes were filled with exhaustion and confusion. 'What are you doing here?' I was so happy to see her.

I glanced apprehensively at Harriet who was retreating backwards to the bedroom door. 'I knew Harriet lived here, I was looking for her actually,' I lied through my teeth. 'Harriet, we were going to meet up soon weren't we, just thought I'd pop round,' I attempted a smile. She didn't go along with the act; she stayed silent as she gripped tightly onto the metal dog lead.

Matt looked down at me sinisterly, 'silly little bitch. Don't lie to me, Harriet would never have told you where she lived, it's too risky. You didn't tell her did you babe?' He turned his head to face her; she shook her head timidly in reply. Why would it be risky? I wondered.

I heard a click from behind his back, I knew straight away that he had a gun, 'look, honestly Harriet is my friend and I found out where she lived that's all, I haven't seen her in a while so I thought I would visit her. I'm sorry for intruding, I'll just leave. She clearly doesn't want to see me today do you hun?' I rambled.
'I'm sorry Brooke,' she whispered as she disappeared with the dog into the bedroom and slammed the door behind her. She was clearly scared to her core of her disgusting boyfriend.

'Na, you can't know this address without being sorted out,' Matt threatened.

'My memory is really bad,' I laughed nervously, 'I won't even remember this address once I leave,'

'You're not going to leave,' he replied as he pulled out the gun and pointed it towards me,'

'No!' Liam cried as he jumped out from behind the sofa, grabbing Matt's hand and pointing the gun away from me, 'Brooke, run!'

'I'm not leaving you!' I argued as I looked around the room for anything I could use to fight Matt off.

'Oh, how sweet,' Matt said as he forcefully hit Liam on the head with the edge of the gun, he fell to the floor next to me, banging his head on the edge of the table. 'Argh,' he let out an awfully loud cry of pain.

Matt made his way towards me next, pulling my hair viciously and throwing me face first up against the wall. 'Maybe I'll have some fun with you while your boyfriend watches,' he sneered, before repeatedly banging my head against the wall.
 I tried to struggle with his grip, but it was so tight I couldn't do anything. My vision blurred as my eyes filled with something liquid-I couldn't tell if it was blood or tears. Matt's hand moved from my hair down to my top as his rough hands slid underneath it. 'Please no,' I begged; I thought I was going to be sick.

'Get off of her!' Liam's voice roared from behind me, I felt Matt being pulled off of me and before I knew it Liam was in front of me with his arms spread wide. 'Don't shoot her, if you're gonna shoot anyone shoot me,' Liam shouted with blood now gushing down his face.

'Liam…' I wept as I attempted to push him out of the way, my vision still blurred.

'I'll shoot you, finish my fun with little peach over there, then shoot her, I'll just have to get two body bags then,' Matt shrugged as if it was no big deal, 'you don't understand, I have no choice!' his voice rumbled around the room.

I thought that was it, there was nothing I could do, Liam and I were both going to die in this crack den and that's how our tragic love story would end.

For a split second time seemed to slow down to a halt. One last time I tried to push Liam away from me and this time I managed to move him, he toppled and fell sideways, just as Matt shot the gun, I felt a sharp pain in my leg and screamed as I fell to the floor-everything went back into full speed as it registered what had just happened. I had just been shot, and I was about to be killed.

The pain was unbearable, Liam-with blood still pouring out from the wound in his head- was helplessly trying to pull me into the kitchen, attempting to get me as far away from Matt as he could, tears were flooding down his bloody face. Matt walked towards us, aiming the gun at my head.

Harriet had now emerged from the bedroom and was screaming something at Matt that I couldn't make out, everything was muffled and blurry to me. I could just about make out Harriet being flung across the room with some force and a loud bang as she landed against the table, her body lay still on the floor.

Liam was still trying to drag me out of the house as Matt pointed the gun back towards my head, but before he could shoot there was a terrible cracking sound and he fell to the floor like a rag doll.

I looked up helplessly, clearing my eyes with my hands. Billy was towering over us holding a baseball bat above his head, a crazed look filled his once kind eyes as he hit him again, and again and again.

'Stop! Billy, stop!' I tried to scream as blood repeatedly splattered against my face.

Liam jumped up and grabbed the bat from Billy's hand, 'fuck man, leave him his dead,' he panted.

Billy looked at the bloody bat in Liam's hand and the battered body lying on the floor by his feet and fell to his knees. Liam ran back to me and pulled his jumper off, wrapping it around my leg.

'Come on, we need to get out of here,' he wheezed as he picked me up and left the house. I was in and out of cautiousness, but I could feel Liam's arms wrapped tightly around me as he carried me back to Billy's car.

I felt the cold leather of the seat on my warm body as he carefully placed me down, I faintly heard him say, 'I'll be back; I need to go get Billy.'

The next thing I remember is being driven away by Liam, his beautiful face was filled with blood and tears and his clothes soaked in what I assumed was my blood, Billy was sitting in the front and they were shouting at each other. Everything was muffled; I couldn't quite make out what was going on around me.

'What are we going to do,' Billy was crying into his hands, 'I killed a man, his dead,'

'You were saving us,' Liam was reassuring him.

I closed my eyes and drained them out. As I opened my eyes again I was being carried into Liam's. I could hear the panicked voices of everyone in the house; I didn't like the noise so I closed my eyes and sang Auntie Veronica's bedtime song to calm everyone down. The last thing I heard was Liam's desperate voice screaming for someone to help me.

I woke up confused of my whereabouts, my eyes were blurry and I felt like I had been hit by a truck. I heard a distant voice saying my name, but I couldn't see anyone around me. Tears began to fall from my eyes and before I knew it I was sobbing hysterically. The voice seemed to get further and further away, I couldn't hear what they were saying anymore. I couldn't hear anything over my cries.

I felt a heavy object hold onto my shoulder, I tried to shake it off but it didn't budge. I grabbed it and realized it was just a hand.

As my eyes adjusted to the light I could see that it was Liam holding me as I cried, 'Liam, don't go,' I begged.

'I'm not going anywhere, just get some rest…' I heard him say as I fell back to sleep.

48 hours later

'You scared me so much B,' Jamie said as she sat down on the bed with a tray of food for me, 'how does your leg feel?'

'My leg?' I looked at her frowning.

'You were shot,' she said slowly. I carried on looking at her with a blank expression, 'you were shot in the leg'

I laughed at her worried expression, 'I know you idiot. Do you think I could forget this? It hurts so much,'

'Well Neil had a friend over who knew how to treat gun shots…' Jamie began.

'…who's Neil?' I interrupted.

'Oh shit, you don't know them do you' she chuckled, 'Neil and Carlos are the most amazing men I've ever met, they seem like characters out of a film or something,'

'Someone's got a crush,' I mocked her through a mouthful of porridge.

'Probably married' she shrugged, 'should I go get Liam and tell him you're awake? He's been worried sick about you B,'

'Does he really want to see me, looking like this?' I uttered.

'What do you mean?' Jamie laughed at me.

'I bet I look like a ghost, my hair hasn't been brushed in god knows how long *and* I stink…' I grimaced as I sniffed under my arms, 'really badly,'

'It's better than the alternative isn't it?' she said as she took the empty bowl from me, 'anyway, Liam worships the ground you walk on, B. Your moisturizing routine could involve smothering pigs shit on your face and he'd still think you were the most beautiful thing on this planet.'

'Can't I get up?' I asked, ignoring her slightly jealous sounding tone. I noticed some crutches and a wheel chair on the other side of the room.

'It's only been like 48 hours since someone *shot* you, don't you think you should wait?' she protested.

'I've been in bed for 2 *days*?' I exclaimed, 'I'm getting up,'

Jamie shook her head in disagreement as I attempted to pull myself to the side of the bed. I felt so weak, but I was determined to carry on as if my leg didn't feel like it was constantly on fire, 'I promised Liam I would help him, I can't break that promise,' I sighed, trying one last time to swing my legs out of bed, 'see, I'm not such a cripple after all.'

Jamie helped me out of bed and into the wheelchair, she wheeled me to the top of the stairs and we looked down them for a second, clueless.

'We didn't think this through did we Jam?' I laughed, trying to hide how much the laugh made me wince.

'It was your idea to get out of bed, don't blame me. Shall I just throw you down there?' she giggled as he rocked the chair backwards and forwards jokingly.

'I could shuffle down on my bum, you know like we used to do as kids,' I suggested.

'B, that idea is almost as stupid as when you decided to dye your hair bright blue,' Jamie laughed as she slid past me and strutted down the stairs, leaving me stranded in the hallway.

'Oh, I see how it is, just leave me I'll be fine on my own!' I called after her as she disappeared into the front room.

When she reappeared again she was joined by a bewildered looking man who I hadn't met yet, 'how the fuck are you even awake, let alone trying to get downstairs,' he laughed as he carefully pulled me out of the wheelchair and carried me down.

'It's boring up there,' I moaned. Flinching as the movement sent a shooting pain through my leg, 'I'm Brooke, who are you?'

'No, you're a fucking hooligan,' he muttered as he carried me into the room, placing me carefully onto the sofa, 'I'm Neil, Liam's friend'

Everyone starred at me with a mixture of disbelief and adoration as I lay back on the sofa, breathing out a huge sigh of relief.

'How are you feeling'?' Dale questioned, handing me a cigarette and lighter.

'Thanks,' I breathed as I took them off him and sparked up, 'I've felt better, not going to lie.'

'I bet, there was so much blood, Nathan nearly fainted when we had to clean it off the floor,' Dale laughed, rustling Nathan's thin, mousy brown hair. I glanced down and noticed one part of the carpet was a lot darker than the rest, I shuddered.

Nathan peered up at me, clearly embarrassed, 'sorry,' I mouthed.

At that moment the back door burst open and Liam sped through the room to kneel by my head, 'Brooke, you okay?' he gasped, but before I could answer he carried on hysterically blurting out words, 'I was so worried…why didn't anyone tell me she was awake? I've been in that room every day, I left for one fag and you wake up… I'm sorry…I didn't leave…I promise…I'm gonna look after you…I'm sorry…are you okay?'

I put my finger on his mouth to shut him up and kissed him like I'd never kissed him before. Everyone in the room awkwardly looked in another direction, and there were a few heaving sounds coming from Jamie, but I didn't care. I was so happy that we had made it out of there alive.

'I'm fine,' I reassured him as I lay back down again, attempting to cover the breathlessness the kiss had caused me.

'Are you sure?' he frowned as I blew smoke towards his direction, 'you shouldn't be smoking, give me that,' he ordered, trying to pull the cigarette from my fingers.

'Stop worrying,' I pleaded, 'obviously it hurts, but at least we all got back alive...' I stopped as I said this. Studying the room I realized Billy wasn't there, 'where's Billy?' I whispered, not sure if I even wanted to know the answer.

I closed my eyes as a memory of the fight flashed through my mind. Billy was hitting Matt again and again. I felt the blood splatter on my face and I put my hands up to wipe it off. Liam narrowed his eyes as I done this, so I pretended that I was scratching forehead and tried to push the memory from my mind.

'Billy's fine babe,' Liam stated as he tucked a strand of my matted, greasy hair behind my ear.

'Is Matt still there?' I hissed, glaring up at Dale as I noticed him watching us talk.

Liam turned his back to Dale and the others and shook his head, 'his in the garden room, in the freezer; you've missed a lot while you've been out. I'll fill you in I promise, but when you're better,'

'Tell me now, I'm going to worry otherwise,' I ordered. There was a knock at the door, Liam jumped up and hurried over to it.

'Liam bought in the big guns,' Dale muttered to me. I was briefly confused by this comment, but when the man walked in I could see exactly what he meant. Neil stood up and greeted the second man. The moment he walked through the door the whole atmosphere in the room changed. There was no other word to describe these two men together other than powerful. The man who walked in was massive; his muscles were showing through his tight, black top. He took his sunglasses off and nodded at us. Neil was just a bit smaller than him, but was still immensely huge compared to the rest of us who had all evolved like normal human beings.

'So where do we start?' Liam laughed anxiously, 'basically after the whole thing at Matt's, I called Neil and Carlos,' he nodded in their direction, as if he was thanking them, 'explained everything to them, they sorted you out with a doctor first of all, that's all I cared about, and then they went back to the house to clean up. Matt is in the freezer, and yeah I think that's it on that whole situation?' he turned to Dale and Nathan as they nervously glanced towards the garden room where the huge freezer was situated.

'Where have you two been?' I asked as I noticed their confusion.

Nathan tilted his head towards me as I spoke like a dog listening to the word treat. 'We came round not long after you were shot because we hadn't heard anything from Liam, we didn't know someone had been killed?' he shot a disproving look in Liam's direction. Dale stayed silent for the first time since I had known him.

'Yeah, while we were sorting everything else out we asked Dale and Nathan if they could clean up the mess, I guess we missed a few minor details out,' Liam shrugged.

'Yeah, just a few minor details,' Dale managed to reply sarcastically, the colour had drained from his usually rosy face, 'so now we are part of a murder cover up?'

Liam looked at him guiltily before turning his attention back to me, he looked exhausted. 'Harriet?' I whispered as I remembered her body flying across the room. 'Do I even want to know what happened to Harriet?'

Liam stoked my arm gently, he hadn't let go of me once since he'd entered the room. 'Harriet wasn't there when they went back, the dog was still in the bedroom but she wasn't there. We took the dog to an animal shelter, said we found him on the street.' I smiled lovingly at him; he was always so kind hearted. 'So hopefully that means she has got as far away from all of this as possible. We have tried calling her, but no luck so far.'

I sat in shock for a minute; I couldn't believe how quickly all of this had escalated. I noticed Jamie was being extremely quiet, I felt sorry for her, if she'd just been shot I would have been a mess too.

Liam continued filling me in, 'Billy's fine, he just wanted to keep out of this house, his being doing stuff for us at home,' he continued to caress my arm as he spoke, 'Carlos is my mum's old friend, the one who found me at home when I was younger, we work together now at his garage,' I nodded, remembering when Liam had first told me the story about his mum; it seemed like another lifetime ago.

'Neil is Rebecca's brother; it turns out that mum and Rebecca were quite good friends, they worked together around the same time…'

I held up my hand to stop Liam talking, 'who is Rebecca? Or am I suffering from memory loss too?'

'Rebecca's name was pinned up on a board in Matt's house and Billy had photos of it on his phone. And I remembered that I'd read about her before, I think I told you that? She was in a car crash and arrested. Neil never mentioned that he was her brother before because she's in prison and they don't speak' I closed my eyes as Liam mentioned Matt and Billy; I couldn't shake the memory of it from my mind.

'I didn't know what good bringing up Georgina would do for Liam either,' Neil added.

As it happens, a hell of a lot had been done while I was recovering. Billy had managed to 'access' -as he ever so innocently put it- Mr. Daniels' phone and email accounts. He'd discovered a few exchanges between Mr. Daniels and Guedo himself, discussing an up and coming trip to Italy that they had booked for the beginning of July. I was utterly confused by everything I was being told, but impressed with myself that I had linked Guedo and Mr. D together so early on.

'So, all we know about Guedo for certain is that he runs a security firm that seems to cater to the very rich. And we know that he is in someway linked to Mr. Daniels who investigates trafficking and organised crime,' Liam carried on, addressing everyone in the room, 'and also that he is my mum's ex boyfriend who has been missing for over 20 years.'

I raised my eyebrows at him, I guessed now was as better time as any to break the news of my epiphany. 'I shouldn't be telling you all this, but we have been told at work that the leader of the organization we're investigating is someone who they refer to as Seven. I'm pretty convinced that it could be Guedo. I think Guedo is the leader, and I think that Mr. D is like a corrupt dirty officer which I only thought existed in films. But we haven't been getting *anywhere* with this case. We've arrested some low in the pecking order druggie waste of spaces but I think stuff is being covered up so we don't have any clear evidence or leads. It's crazy, but it isn't impossible that they would have someone on the inside who is covering their tracks is it?' Once I'd said it out loud, I realized how ridiculous I probably sounded, 'I know it's a bit far-fetched, but since being shot I guess that means that pretty much anything is possible right?'

'How long have you been holding onto that genius idea?' Liam glared at me in astonishment.

'So what does your sister have to do with this?' I asked Neil. Neil sighed as if he had told this story a million times, 'my sister was put in prison for life for the attempted murder of Guedo. She was friends with Georgina, Georgina was dating Guedo, there was some sort of argument in a car, I don't know, I'm a bad brother and I didn't go to the trials, I thought she'd done it, he clearly brainwashed me too,'

'This was 1994, the year mum died again,' Liam whispered.

'Rebecca would be 46 now,' I sighed, 'I can't imagine being in prison for all of those years.'

'Knowing you're innocent as well,' Liam added. Then it hit me, the notebook I had found in Harriet and Matt's house mentioned something about seven moving abroad.

'Where is the notebook I found in the house?' I ordered.

Liam shrugged, 'Billy probably has it, why?'

'I found Harriet's notes, it looked like Matt had been telling her stuff about the company, it said that Seven was due to move abroad soon, it isn't a coincidence that Guedo and Mr. Daniels are going on a trip to Italy is it?' I rambled.

Everyone was silent, I could see the concerned expressions painted on their faces and I wondered if they too felt like we had bitten off more than we could chew. We sat in silence for a while and then another crazy thought hit me, 'what if she isn't dead?'

'Who isn't dead?' Liam shot a look at me with that intrigued glint in his eyes again.

'Georgina, your mum, what if your mum isn't dead?' I winced as I became a little bit too excited. I wondered if I should have kept this brain wave to myself, but he was eagerly waiting for an explanation, 'you say they never found her body, it was never officially reported that she is dead, Liam! She might not be? Maybe she has been taken, held captive somewhere. Or she fled because she got in too deep with it all? I remember now, her picture isn't on that wall along with Rebecca and Britney and all of those other people, why not? Maybe she got away!' I could feel the wheels in my brain turning around yet again; it was good to be back.

'I think I'd rather her be dead than held somewhere,' Liam murmured.

Yes, it's still March!

We walked into the square, grey room. I clung onto my crutches tightly, 'its fine,' Liam reassured me, 'don't be scared'

'Of course she's going to be bloody scared you idiot,' Jamie argued, 'I don't see why you're doing this B, if you two get caught here who knows what Mr. Daniels will do, should have just let me and Billy come,'

'Now, now children,' Neil rolled his eyes. The truth is I wasn't scared at all, I was just in so much pain that I thought if I let go of Liam or the crutch I would never be able to get back up again. But if they thought I was scared, I'd rather them believe that than worry about me even more than they already did. Liam hadn't left my side for the past few days and they were adamant that I should have just stayed in bed. But somehow, here I was, still alive and still wanting to do everything in my power to help Liam-no matter the cost.

We followed Neil's lead as he sat down at a large metal table in the corner of the brightly lit room. We all squeezed onto a bench on one side of the table. I studied the room cautiously as we waited, there were 10 other benches placed around the room and each one was filled with people waiting just like us. I could sense the despairing mood of every single person, waiting longingly for their loved ones to come out from behind the door just to see them for a short period of time.

After what seemed like an age, the heavy, grey door clunked open and the guard started to let the prisoners into the room.

They were all wearing grey tracksuits with yellow bibs placed over the top. Right at the back was a skinny, fatigued looking lady. She had brown, wiry hair and her skin was wrinkly and pale-Rebecca.

She looked up as the guard pointed to our table. Her eyes seemed to light up when she spotted Neil. She slowly made her way over to the table we were sitting at. I tensed up with nerves, but Jamie and Liam seemed fine.

'Rebecca,' Liam said confidently as she sat down, he held out his hand that I wasn't clinging onto for her to shake.

She didn't acknowledge his reached out hand so he put it back under the table, 'who are you?' she asked in a croaky voice, leaning back in her chair and crossing her arms, 'and Neil, it's been a while, what do *you* want?' The moment of joy caused by seeing people seemed to have passed just as quickly as it came.

'The truth,' Liam remained calm and collected, clearly not put off by her rudeness, 'the truth about Guedo.'

Rebecca rolled her eyes, 'like telling a few kids the truth is going to help me, Neil, who are these children?'

'Well these *kids* know a lot more about Guedo than most people, he killed my mum so you start talking,' Liam lowered his voice.

Neil nodded at her, 'they are fine, Rebecca, just help us yeah?'

Rebecca stared suspiciously at us, looking Liam up and down before sitting forwards and putting her frail arms on the table, 'okay, what do you *need* to know?' she asked, her eyes jolted around the room, looking for anyone who might have been listening.

'How do you know Guedo?' Jamie piped up.

'How do I know Guedo?' she sniggered sarcastically, 'I wish I'd never met the bastard'

Neil exhaled heavily, 'I knew this would be a waste of time. You've never told me anything so why would you tell them,'

Rebecca's sunken eyes grew wide as Neil spoke, 'I never told you anything because you never come to see me Neil,' she murmured.

Neil shot her an apologetic look; I wondered why they had grown so far apart. 'I'll tell you, you've come all of this way. I worked as an NCA officer with my friend Georgina, who I'm guessing is your mum?' she glanced at Liam as she said this; he nodded in reply, 'ok this little visit makes sense now.' She commented.

'We worked there for a few years, we were really good friends, then she started dating Guedo. I told her right from the start he was bad news, she kept skipping days at work, would go missing for days…' I watched Liam's face drop, all this time he had thought that his mum was working nights and overtime to provide a better life for them, when really she was leaving him alone to go off with her abusive boyfriend. Rebecca and Georgina's situation seemed to resemble my current one with Harriet, apart from we'd taken care of her abusive boyfriend for her. My mind wondered to where Harriet could be, but I knew this wasn't the time or place for day dreams; I needed to be there for Liam. I squeezed his hand as I didn't know what I could say to him in that moment to make anything better.

He didn't say a word as he carried on listening to Rebecca's story, holding back the tears. '…we were all really worried about her. We were working a big child trafficking case at work, it was traumatizing and I don't know if that got to her, with you being so young and all. I popped round a few times, when you were really little actually, tried to talk her out of seeing Guedo. I told her she wasn't acting like herself, leaving her little one home alone and not showing up for work. It was like she was brainwashed. Anyway, one day Guedo overheard me telling her to leave him; he pleaded with me that if I got to know him I would realise that he wasn't all that bad,'

Neil shuffled in his seat, 'Rebecca, why didn't you tell me any of this? I knew George, I could have helped.'

'What good were you going to do? You were drugged up and in your little gang at that time Neil, if it wasn't for Carlos you'd be dead in a ditch somewhere,' she snapped.

Neil didn't reply, he just looked down at the table shamefully. I felt sorry for him, it must have been hard visiting his sister when she'd been behind bars for so many years and looked so different to when she had first been put away, even I could tell the difference in her and I'd only seen old photographs.

'*Anyway,*' Rebecca continued, 'I agreed to go to lunch with them. I drove us to the local pub and we had some food there, he was pleasant enough and I thought maybe I'd overreacted a bit; maybe she was just acting like a woman madly in love.

After a few hours I got back into the car to drive us home, I started to feel really weird half way and insisted I needed to pull over. I was dizzy, felt sick and my vision was blurry. I couldn't find anywhere to pull over and was begging for Georgina to help me, when I turned around to the back seat she wasn't there,'

Liam frowned, 'she wasn't in the car the whole time? How could you not know, I don't get it?'

Rebecca sighed, 'I don't know what happened, I don't know where she went, I could have sworn she was in the car with us when we left, but Guedo told me he'd spiked my drink. The next thing I remember he was grabbing hold of the steering wheel and we were veering off of the road into a tree.

I was arrested for driving under the influence and he later made a statement that I'd driven into the tree on purpose because we were arguing. He told the court how he had told me he was going to leave me for another woman and I said that we would both die before that happened.'

A tear filled her tired eyes, she wiped it away before it could even fall, 'people believed the story, that we were a *couple*. Of course there was CCTV of us leaving together,'

'And mum wasn't in the CCTV footage?' Liam queried.

Rebecca shook her head, 'they only showed the footage of us leaving in the trial, and it was just Guedo and I, she was nowhere to be seen.'

'Do you remember what date this was?' I piped in.

'Of course, it was Thursday 1st December, 1994,' Rebecca stated matter-of-factly.

'The day before…' I began.

'The day before Britney was murdered?' Rebecca finished my sentence, 'I know, I thought that was weird as well. It was like Guedo was tying up any lose ends before he disappeared…' The guard walked past our table and Rebecca smiled, 'oh that's so lovely darling, I'm so happy your exams went well, I'm so proud…' the smile dropped as soon as he walked away. She paused, studying our shocked expressions intensely.

There was a long moment of silence as we all took in what she had just said, 'he is sick,' Rebecca added bluntly, 'all he cares about is getting what he wants, and he will do anything to get it.'

Liam fidgeted in his seat and pulled my hand closer onto his lap.

'5 minutes left of visiting time,' the guard boomed from across the room. He was looking at our table suspiciously so I began to smile at Rebecca attempting to look as though I had known her for more than 20 minutes.

'Do you have any idea what happened to my mum, any idea at all?' Liam pleaded.

Rebecca shook her head, 'I'm sorry, I know you thought I'd have all the answers but I really don't. If she stayed with him, then she's more than likely dead honey,' I felt Liam's hand begin to shake as tears filled in his eyes.

Again, it hit me just how big this situation I had got involved with was. I was sitting in a prison speaking to a woman who had been convicted for attempted murder, I was putting all of my trust in a boy I hadn't known for very long at all, my leg still had a very painful bullet wound in it, I felt like I was in a film, I just hoped this film had a happy ending.

The guard began to walk over to us, 'we will do everything we can prove your innocence Miss Stevens,' I smiled at her, realising Liam was too choked up to say anything else.

'Well I won't hold my breath, but thank you. Just please be careful,' she said sternly to all of us. She nodded to Neil, who nodded back slowly, before standing up and making her way back out of the room to her cell. I felt an overwhelming sense of sadness for her.

April
It was fast approaching Easter time, the weather was warmer and the sun was shining for longer, but I felt as though I couldn't escape from the darkness.

It had been nearly 3 weeks since the incident at Matt's house and I was still suffering severely from the trauma of it all, both mentally and physically. As I sat across from Dr. Daw I wanted to blurt out everything that had happened. I wanted to tell her how scared I was and how much pain I was in. I wanted to explain the terrors I'd been having every night and how I couldn't close my eyes without experiencing flashbacks of Billy repeatedly smashing Matt's skull. Above all, I wanted to explain how it was all worth it because I was deeply, dangerously and unconditionally in love.

But instead, I just answered her routine questions and lied through my teeth about everything. I had worn the baggiest jogging bottoms I could find so that the swollen wound on my leg would be hidden well. I was still limping and my leg was severely scarred from where the dodgy doc had cut out the bullet. This meant that I had to invent a story about falling over in a pair of heels and being impaled by a broken metal fence. It was easy to spin that story to my family, who I had been speaking to on the odd occasion. As soon as I told them it had happened whilst I was drunk my mum saw that as a perfect opportunity to lecture me on my life choices and the dangers of alcohol. I had practiced my 'I'm okay' smile in the mirror a million times before meeting with Dr. Daw that day.

'My friends convinced me that I should talk to my mum again, said life is too short and all that.' In reality there had been many arguments with Jamie and Liam, they had both drilled into me that I needed to be on speaking terms with my family.

'B, you were shot for fuck sake!' Jamie had shouted at me, 'if that doesn't make you want to see your family then what will?'

So that's really what happened, my friends had convinced me.

'My mum took me apologizing and wanting to be in contact again as a sign of 'change' and as much as I hate seeing her again, it's really nice to see the twins and my dad.'

'You said the word change with some disgust then, I'm just wondering, do you not see change as a good thing?' Dr. Daw questioned insightfully as always.

'I don't think change is a bad thing, I just don't think I've changed,' I retorted bluntly.

'It's been a few weeks since our last session, has anything changed since then?' she inquired in her soft, reassuring voice. She had this great skill of making it sound like she really truly wanted to know the answer to every question she asked. I wondered as I examined her face, if she was mentally making a shopping list for later, or if she was wondering what to have for dinner and that like most people, she really wasn't interested in the answer to her question at all.

Obviously an immense amount had changed, but I couldn't express it all to her. So I told her the parts that I was allowed to speak about.

'I mean, Jamie and I have started renting an apartment, its closer to my boyfriend's house as well so that's nice. We spend a lot of time together all of us, and his friends. So that's changed, I have a better group of friends now.' I replied.

I wasn't lying there; I liked my new social life. Liam and I spent a lot of time at his house, with the usual gang, it was nice.

'But I think my mum thinks I've changed as a person, when really I've just toned myself down around her, to be the version of me she can tolerate, because quite frankly I've had enough arguments with her to last a lifetime and I cannot be bothered to deal with any more now.'

Mrs. Daw nodded, and wrote some notes in her book, before closing it and leaning forwards in her chair, 'but what I'm worried about is the fact that you have to tone yourself down for others, you should be authentically you and nothing else. Is there anyone you can be the real Brooke with?'

I thought about it for a second and sighed, it was a good question, 'I mean who is the real Brooke really though Mrs. Daw? For my mum, no, I could never be myself whatever that is. Around my best friend I'm the quiet one, the one that agrees with what she says and does what she wants to do, around my auntie I'm still the little vulnerable girl who needs looking after…' I stopped as I thought about who I really was. I wasn't expecting to go so deep and meaningful in this session.

'And your boyfriend, you haven't mentioned who you can be when you're around your boyfriend?' Mrs. Daw enquired. I thought for a second, I thought back to all of the time that Liam and I spend alone, and how confident and alive I felt, I couldn't stop myself from smiling.

'Ahh,' Dr. Daw grinned, 'I like him for you, it's not often we see our Brooke crack a smile,' she winked.

'I suppose he brings the best out in me, as cliché as that sounds. I mean, I don't have better manners, or a better sense of maturity, or make better life decisions or whatever else it is that my mother and this world expect of me,' I paused as Dr. Daw picked up her glass of water and took an annoyingly loud slurp, 'but he doesn't seem to care about all of that stuff, that's not important to him.' I continued.

'He makes me want to dance on tables, hug strangers, take risks, he makes me want to live and not just survive, which as you know, I've never done. I've spent my whole life on auto pilot, just surviving and getting through every shitty thing that comes my way and acting exactly how I was always expected to act. I've never truly lived.'

It was only then that I realized how many years of my life I had wasted. In that second I wanted to run out of that room and straight into Liam's arms.

One evening after another unnerving day at work with no advancements and still under the watchful eye of Mr. Daniels, I made my way back to Liam's house. There were a few unfamiliar cars parked on the driveway. I could faintly see a few people pacing up and down his front room. As I entered the room I immediately relaxed, it was just Billy, Dale, Nathan and Chris. Liam looked up at me, he was frowning and seemed worried, but he carried on his conversation with Billy without even saying hello to me.

'Have you found something?' I asked as I sat down; peering over at Billy's laptop. I noticed they were looking through the recordings of Mr. Daniels that we had obtained.

Somehow they had roped me into planting hidden cameras of which Billy had 'borrowed' from work. I had screwed them into the light bulbs of his office so we could keep an eye on what was going on. I had thought it was pretty crazy at the time, but Billy said they couldn't be traced back to anyone if he found them-which we'd all said he probably would seeing as it was a major criminal investigations unit-but we were in so deep what were a few more risks to add to the list?

'Well, we think so,' Billy stuttered, he had recently got some braces fitted and had the funniest lisp I'd ever heard-it was hard to take him seriously.

Liam leaned over to the laptop and pressed the play button, still anxiously studying me, 'What?' I mouthed at him, but he just gestured his head towards the screen where Mr. Daniels was marching up and down his office with his mobile phone glued to his ear.

'…But I don't know what to do, she's just a girl…' he was stammering nervously. My heart sank; I knew straight away he must have been talking about me. Why else would Liam seem so on edge?

'…Yes I know…but…I don't think she knows anything…why sir…of course…yes…okay, I'll get it done…' the phone call ended and he held his head in his hands, he seemed distressed-he was shaking and still walking around his room helplessly-then he retrieved his bag and left.

'So, what does that mean?' I looked at Billy and Liam, confused, 'it was just a phone call, and they could have been talking about anyone. He wasn't necessarily talking to Guedo…' Liam stopped me.

'Brooke, have you spoken to Jamie today?' he asked me slowly. The rest of the boys in the room went silent; I looked around noticing that Jamie wasn't there.

'Where's Jamie?' I stood up, glaring at each and every jittery person in the room, 'what do you all know?'

There was silence, no one was telling me anything. My heart was racing, tears filled my tired eyes and I felt a lump grow in my throat, 'please, just tell me…where is she?' I pleaded with them as my voice cracked.

Liam stood up and led me into the kitchen, 'Babe…'

'Don't babe me Liam! Just tell me where she is!' I shouted, tears began streaming down my face.

'We don't know...' he looked at me apprehensively.

'You don't know...how can you not know? You have been *filming* him, you have a fucking genius sitting in there who could probably rob a million pounds from a bank if he felt the urge to, but you *don't know* how Jamie has suddenly just disappeared into thin air?'

Liam tried to calm me down, but I hobbled with us much force as I could back into the front room, my leg was throbbing from driving home and that hadn't made it any better. I was angry, but not at them. I was angry at myself for getting Jamie caught up in this.

'Look, we dunno if they have taken her, you know what she's like, she is probably at a boy's house,' Dale tried to console me.

'What she's *like*? You've known her for 5 seconds; you know nothing about what she is like!' I shouted at him. I was the only person who was allowed to make those sorts of jokes about her.

'Yeah, we've known her 5 seconds and nearly all of us have spent the night at hers,' Dale argued back.

They all sniggered like little school boys, 'You think this is a joke?' I screamed, trying my best to charge at Dale, my leg buckled and I fell to the floor with a thump, 'She's gone and you think this is fucking funny!' I carried on, struggling to stand up again. They sat there silently, looking at each other with a guilty expression on their face.

'Dale, leave it out,' Liam shouted as he dropped to the floor next to me, holding my trembling body as tight as he could.

'I'm sorry man, we're just as upset as her,' Dale muttered.

I gave up with my attempt to stand up and clutched onto my burning leg, 'You are not just as upset as me! She has been my best friend for my whole life!' Liam pulled me into his chest as I sobbed uncontrollably through the pain, 'she's my best friend, Liam. What have we done?'

My vision began to blur and my ears started to ring, it was like being back in Matt and Harriet's front room all over again. I could faintly hear Liam telling me to stay awake, but it was too late.

'JAMIE!' I screamed as I shot up. I noticed I was on Liam's sofa with a blanket slung over me, my forehead was dripping with sweat and my leg still felt as though it was on fire.

Liam jumped up from the floor, his curls were a mess and his eyes were tired, 'It's okay, I'm here, I'm here.'

'What happened?' I asked softly as tears fell from my eyes, 'is she still missing?'

Liam looked at me apologetically as he switched the lamp on, 'The boys haven't stopped looking, and we'll find her. But you need to focus on getting better.'

'There's nothing wrong with me,' I snapped.

'There is, your leg is infected, doc came last night when you fainted and checked you over, his prescribed you some antibiotics to fight the infection, but you have to rest babe, please,'

'How can I rest, Liam? Would you?' I protested

'If you asked me to, yes I would,' he caressed my hand, 'this is serious; you need to get better for me okay?'

I nodded stubbornly and fell back onto the cushions. I couldn't believe what had become of my life. I stayed up most of the night with the news on, calling Jamie and looking on the internet for any reports of a girl being found. It started to rain around 4am. Each tap of rain against the window signified another second that I was sat on that bed and Jamie hadn't been found.

It was around 11am a few days later when I was awoken by a knock at Liam's door. He climbed off of the sofa of which we had slept on most nights and gently opened the door, hushing whoever was on the other side so they wouldn't wake me up.

There were some faint deep sounding mutters before the boys tip toed into the front room. I sat up and gave them a half-hearted smile.

'Sorry if we woke you,' Chris smiled back at me as Liam opened the curtains.

'And sorry about the other day,' Dale added.

'Yeah, Sorry…' Nathan mimicked.

'Me too,' I sighed as I shuffled in my seat, 'emotions are all over the place at the moment, but we all need each other, we can't be fighting right now.'

'You don't have to say sorry,' Chris assured me, 'it was our fault,'

Nathan nodded in agreement, 'Honestly, we're sorry for being so stupid,'

Dale smiled at me, 'We will find her, we love Jamie to bits, just like we love you,'

Billy turned to face us; he had massive black bags under his eyes, 'have you not been sleeping?' I asked him sympathetically.

He shook his head, 'I have been looking into every way possible to help you find Jamie,' he yawned, 'and there's something else…'

'What?' I stared warily at him.

'I could most defiantly rob a bank if I wanted to, but my mother never bought me up to be a notorious bank robber, so I'd like it if you didn't hold that one against me please,'

I looked at him and burst out laughing as I realised he was referring to my statement about his genius state of mind, and then everyone else began to laugh through their exhaustion too.

I looked around the room and a wave of emotion soured over me, 'thank you everyone, you have been such good mates to me, I'm so glad I met you all,' No one answered, they all just smiled at me with the same emotional look I knew I had on my face, Liam fixed his eyes to mine lovingly and I knew everything would eventually be okay.

After another hopeless day of attempting to find out where Jamie was, Liam and I had reluctantly taken ourselves to bed. It was nice that the antibiotics had finally begun to do their thing and I could hobble upstairs and sleep in a comfortable bed for the first time that week. Everyone had left feeling just as deflated as us.

'Maybe we should just call the police Liam,' I suggested nervously, 'I don't know what else we can do, we're out of our depth here,'

Liam pulled me onto his chest and kissed my head, 'I know, I was thinking the same thing. This is all because of me and it turns out my mum just didn't care about me. All of this was for nothing,'

'You don't know that,' I answered reassuringly as I wrapped my arm around his stomach, 'everyone makes mistakes,' I jumped as that moment my phone rang very loudly, my heart was in my mouth, could this be Jamie?

'It's 1 in the morning, who's calling you?' Liam frowned as the light from my phone shone in his tired eyes.

'Unknown caller,' I whispered, jolting upwards, 'hello?' I answered anxiously.

A deep voice bellowed down the other end of the phone. 'I'm assuming this is your little device I found in the light in my office, Brooke? No one else who works here is quite as deranged as you.'

My heart sank, 'Mr. Daniels?' Liam jumped out of bed quickly chucking some clothes he had thrown on the floor on, he gestured for me to give him the phone but I shook my head, 'I just want to know where Jamie is, that's all, then we'll leave this alone,'

'No, you won't,' he argued, 'you can come and get her if you want, I can tell you where she is, but I doubt you'll leave alive,'

Liam was fumbling around in the wardrobe for a pair of shoes, *where are you going?* I mouthed to him.

'Just tell me where she is, please. We haven't gone to the police even though I know a lot more than you think, trust me.' I attempted to sound threatening, but my voice cracked and I just sounded like a shaky mess.

'They are transporting to Italy soon, she'll be long gone…' he began.

'I know that,' I snapped, 'I've known about your trip to Italy for months,'

'Well then I guess you know that you're too late,' Mr. Daniels replied smugly. I frowned at Liam as he paced up and down the room frantically.

My anger was building the more I heard how confident he was about winning this sick little game, 'I know about you and I know about Guedo and Brittany and Rebecca and Georgina, about the *trafficking* about the drugs, I know everything and if you think we are going to sit back and let this carry on you're wrong Mr. D,' I hung up as he began to laugh. 'Liam, where are you going?' I shouted as he continued to walk widths of the room.

'I don't know, I panicked, I thought he was gonna tell us where she was, did he?'

I shook my head, 'but I think I've just dropped us in it,'

'Brooke, we've been in it for the past year, who gives a fuck,' Tears filled my eyes, 'we still don't know where she is,' Liam's phone began to buzz on the bedside table.

'Bill?' Liam answered hysterically, 'yeah…yeah she just got a phone call… yeah it was that prick… you've done that to all of our phones? Shit Bill you're a genius, yeah…yeah we're coming now.' Liam hung up and his crazed eyes starred at me, 'so Billy has all our phones tapped, his traced that call you just got, we're gonna find her B!'

'I'm coming, don't even try and talk me out of it…' I shouted.

'I couldn't even if I wanted to,' Liam reassured me as he pulled me out of bed and helped me dressed. He brushed my knotted hair gently and wrapped his arms around my waist for a moment, 'we will find her, okay?'

It was about 2AM by the time everyone had arrived at Billy's house, 'The phone call came from an industrial estate in Brixton, so not too far from us at all. Whether he is still there now I don't know, but it's worth a try,' he briefed us all, 'we ready?'

'Let's get these fuckers,' Carlos hollered powerfully.

Liam jumped off of the sofa, 'do you think we will be able to save her Liam?' I asked, following him as quickly as I could as he rushed out into the hallway.

'Course we are gonna Brooke, look at the people we have on our side,' I noticed Liam was rummaging through a big, black rucksack to check he had everything he needed one last time, I peered in and noticed a small laptop, his phone and a knife. I knew it was necessary, but the thought of Liam fighting anyone with a knife scared me to the core.

Billy followed us out, 'The plans a solid one Brooke, we will be fine, just everyone remember to have the phones and lights ready on my signal,'

'Remind me what your signal is again, Billy?' Neil laughed, 'a bird noise?'

'No it's not a *bird noise*, It's a text message, please don't be listening out for the mating call of a dove because you will *not* hear one,' Billy barked in response to Neil's tomfoolery.

Neil held his hands in the air jokingly, 'No pigeon mating calls, got it,'

'What do we do now?' I asked Liam. I was uncomfortably squeezed between the huge units that were Carlos and Neil in the back of Billy's not so big *Ford Fiesta*. We thought taking Carlo's huge range rover would draw too much attention.

My phone clock flashed to **2:47AM.** It was still extremely dark outside, but we could make out the figures of a few men parked in the desolate industrial estate.

'Well they are still here, something must be going down tonight,' Liam speculated.

'Are there lots of them?' I breathed, trying to make out as many figures as I could.

'There's probably a fucking army of them,' Carlos grunted, not being one to sugar coat things, ever.

Billy turned around to face us all from the driver's seat, 'so we are all clear on what we are doing yes? Neil you're off on that direction,' he pointed left towards what looked like some old scaffolding surrounding a derelict building, 'Carlos, you're the opposite direction to Neil. Liam and I are going to try get as close as we can to them, just cover us, please,' Billy paused, raising his eyebrows at Carlos and Neil. Carlos pulled a gun out from his back pocket and Neil followed lead.

'Don't worry Bill,' Neil reassured, 'we have you covered,'

'Take these,' Billy handed them some round bulbs that looked like they belonged to a police car. I wondered how many things Billy had actually stolen from his work and how they hadn't noticed yet. They both took the lights before creeping out of the car to their assigned spots.

Liam looked at me with a concerned expression on his face, 'you're gonna hate me for saying this, but Brooke you need to stay in here,'

'Liam, I love you, but I am coming with you and Billy, I need to see this through to the end.' I insisted. He knew there was no arguing with me when it came to Jamie, it was a battle he would always lose.

We snuck as close as we could possibly get to where the men were standing. I noticed there were several large cars and one very long loading lorry. The headlights from the cars lit up a few of the figures faces as they stood in a circle; they seemed to be waiting for something.

There was a man leaning up against a shiny, black Range Rover. He was big, bigger than Carlos, bigger than anyone I had ever seen before. He took a pull of his cigarette and chucked it on the floor, he turned around and I gasped as the light revealed the scar that I had seen in so many photographs, the scar that covered the length of his face and travelled over his eye. 'Guedo,' I whispered to myself.

After about 10 minutes, Guedo's attention turned to a smaller car arriving. It stopped next to where the others were parked. I watched as a man appeared from the driver's seat, he was dragging someone towards the big group of men. I closed my eyes as I realized who it was. I felt Liam's hand squeeze mine, I felt so scared for Jamie.

Billy's whisper came from the other side of me, 'Brooke, open your eyes, we need all eyes on Jamie while this goes down. I noticed that he was tapping away at the small laptop Liam had packed and knew that the time had come.

The man who had Jamie threw her to the floor where Guedo was standing; her head was right by his feet. I felt sick. Then, he pulled out a gun and held it to her head. She screamed. I went to jump up, but Liam pulled me back down again.

'I'm sorry, you can't. We have it under control,' he insisted. I knew I had to do what he said. I wanted to swap places with her, it was entirely my fault. I looked next to me and watched Billy as he was still quickly tapping the keyboard.

A few seconds after Billy had stopped typing there were the sound of police sirens from where Neil and Carlos had situated themselves. The blue lights lit up the area and I ducked lower against the storage container we were hiding behind. Guedo and his men looked at each other, terrified. They jumped back into their cars and revved up their engines ready to leave. Guedo was shouting, 'drive!'

Jamie was still on the floor, I could hear her sobs. Guedo had given the gun to another man who was holding it to her head, but pleading helplessly for them to let him in the car. Liam pulled out his phone and took a photo of all the number plates he could get as they drove away.

When all the cars had left Carlos and Neil stood up and ran over to the man they had left behind, pulling out their guns from their back pockets.

Liam breathed a sigh of relief and hugged me tightly, 'it worked, and you're okay'.

Carlos was shouting at the man, 'we are the police, drop your weapon and hold your hands over your head,'

The man dropped his gun as instructed and Neil grabbed him before leading him back over to where we had parked. I wondered what they were going to do with him, holding someone captive hadn't been part of the original plan.

As soon as the coast was clear I was off, I hobbled over to Jamie as quickly as I could and grabbed her; she was trembling and couldn't move. Her face was battered black and blue. Tears were running down her bruised cheeks as she fell into my arms.

'I'm so sorry,' I whispered repeatedly. Liam and I put our arms around her and led her back to the car.

Billy shouted from behind us, 'guys wait!' I turned back around to see him attempting to open the doors of the lorry they had left behind. Neil ran over to help him and eventually they forced it open. Liam and I placed Jamie into the back seat of the car and looked at each other with relief, but not for long.

'Oh my god,' Billy shrieked.

'It's okay, it's okay, we're not going to hurt you,' I could hear Neil saying over and over again. I knew straight away what they had found.

Carlos drove us back to Liam's house while Neil stayed to sort out the new situation we had found ourselves in. I looked at Jamie, she was still trembling. I had my arm around her tightly as she was leaning her head on my chest. My heart broke as I looked at her black eye and cut face, I didn't know how she could go anywhere near me.

I turned the other way and whispered to Liam, 'thank you,' He looked at me; his curly hair was blowing in the wind from the open window. My heart fluttered.

The man we had somehow managed to kidnap was squirming around in the boot. I could hear his muffled cries for help from behind me.

'Alright,' Carlos and Neil nodded at me as I walked in the room.

I nodded back at them, picking up my cigarette box, 'You okay?'

'Yep, we're just talking about what to do with Ricky boy in there,' Carlos snickered.

They had taken him out of the boot and into the garden room, tying him up on a chair. I wondered how they could be so calm and still manage to laugh with everything that had transpired that night.

It was now 11AM and I hadn't slept a wink. I spent the night helplessly staring at Jamie and her battered face. She had passed out as soon as her head hit the pillow and was still asleep now.

'What are we gonna do about him?' Liam asked as he walked over to me and placed a reassuring kiss on my forehead. I sparked a cigarette and stretched my legs out in front of me, realising I'd taken on a lot of Liam's traits without even realising.

'I dunno' Neil shrugged, 'isn't that what Billy is for. You know, the thinking and shit,'

'Neil, what happened to those people in the back of the van?' I asked, not sure if I even wanted to know the answer.

Neil looked at me apologetically, 'not everyone was alive. We called the police, anonymously of course,' he glanced towards Billy as he said this, reassuring him that he had thought of everything. 'So I'm guessing you'll hear about that at work?'

'Probably, if Mr. Daniels even lets me through the door, what am I going to do?' I wondered.

'Are you okay Brooke?' Liam scanned my face.

'No I'm not okay,' I responded, 'I'm angry, how are things like this still happening?' a tear fell down my cheek, but I brushed it away. I wasn't going to continue being the girl who cried and let everybody else come to the rescue anymore. I didn't want to continue feeling scared and letting my anxiety rule my life. I was already so far removed from the girl that Liam had met nearly a year ago. I needed to continue becoming the new Brooke, the fearless and adventurous Brooke; I liked her a lot better.

'Right, I'm gonna take this tape off of your mouth mate, make a sound and trust me, you will never be able to make one again, okay?' Carlos threatened.

The man named Ric was sitting on a garden chair in the middle of the room, he had his legs tied to the chair and was clinging on to a half drunken bottle of water. He nodded in reply to Carlos.

Neil patrolled around the man and ripped off the tape, he breathed in and out deeply, gasping for air.

Liam, Jamie and I were sitting on turned over boxes near the door. He starred at Jamie with a disgusted look on his face, 'don't even look at her,' I demanded, 'why are we letting him have bottles of water, we don't care if he dies of dehydration do we?'

'Come 'ere den 'nd say tha' to ma face, yo ugly bitch,' he sneered; he had a strong Italian accent. His voice was horrible and rough-the sort of voice that went straight through you. His dirty brown hair was stuck to his face from the amount he was sweating and as he opened his mouth to speak I noticed he hardly had any teeth, and the teeth he did have were as black as coal.

Carlos strolled towards him, 'didn't I just say, do not speak?' he said in a patronising tone. He bent down so his face was right up against the man's before he jolted up and punched him. Ric lent back in the chair and spat blood. Carlos- turning his back to the man and walking towards the back wall of the room where a variety of tools were hanging- remained calm and collected. I sniggered as Ric flinched every time Carlos moved his hand towards a tool. I was enjoying it, which surprised me.

Neil looked at me as I laughed and joined in, 'I think someone is scared don't you Brooke?'

'I non get'a scared!' he shouted; Carlos walked casually towards him again.

'I told you not to Talk, Ric. And you're talking. Only talk when we ask you a question, yeah?' Carlos hit him again. After Ric had recovered from the second blow, he nodded and didn't say another word, eyes filled with fear and his head bowing to the floor.

Carlos paced around the chair and stopped behind him. Ric attempted to turn around, but failed as the chair nearly toppled over.

I laughed again, 'he has a gun to your head darling,' I smiled mockingly at him. Liam and Jamie starred at me in astonishment.

'B!' Jamie whispered, 'what's gotten into you?'

Carlos smirked at me, 'Brooke, come here,' he gestured with his head, I stood up and limped over to where Ric was sitting, 'tell him why we have him. I think this dumb little shit needs everything spelled out for him.'

'Gladly,' I beamed; I was really getting into it. I wondered if that made me a bit evil.

I looked down at Ric cowering in the chair-cowering because of me-a 24 year old girl who had been wrapped up in cotton wool and told what to do by her parents her whole life. A 24 year old girl who had grown up surrounded by snobby, 'educated' people and I realized; we weren't educated at all, at least not in the important things. Yes, I could tell you the capital of most countries, and solve a math equation in a few minutes. I could be polite and look 'presentable,' I knew the routine to the Nutcracker from my ballet lessons and I knew how to play the piano, but none of that compares to what I had learnt during the short time I'd known Liam.

He had taught me that I could do anything I put my mind to, that I could easily look after myself and not need anyone's assistance. Most importantly, Liam and the boys had taught me what a real family should be. They had taught me what it was like to look out for other people without them even having to ask, I had learnt so much about the type of person I actually wanted to be-not the person I was told to be.

I felt a rush of adrenaline, I felt powerful. I leaned over Ric, one hand on each arm of the chair and spoke quietly, 'you are gonna tell us every little detail you know okay. Don't you dare leave anything out because we *will* find out. We are a lot smarter than you and all your other little friends give us credit for, but wait they aren't your friends are they? Because if they were, they wouldn't have left you to finish their dirty work, and I don't really think they will be sending out a search party any time soon, do you?'

I pulled a chair out and placed it so the back was facing Ric; I swung my legs around it and sat down, 'first, you took my best friend, why?'

There was silence for a few seconds as Ric starred me blankly in the eyes, 'I'll ask again, why did you take her?' Still no answer, I moved my chair out of the way and walked over to the wall covered in tools. I studied it languidly before reaching up for a hammer; I swung it around and shrugged, 'suppose this will do,'

Still, silence. 'You nearly *killed* an innocent girl. For god sake you *have* killed hundreds of innocent people. So if *you* kill, isn't it okay for *me* to?' I looked at the hammer before looking back at him; I noticed everyone was gazing at me in awe.

Of course I wasn't going to kill him-I could never kill anyone-not after how traumatized I was by witnessing Billy take a life. But scaring him into thinking I was mad and deranged enough to? That was a lot of fun.

'Ok, ok I talk, I talk,' he jabbered. I pulled back the garden chair and took a seat once more. 'Guedo tell us to keep eye on you all, 'cause you had people looking into him…Mr. D had told him about you all.'

'…what does Mr. Daniels have to do with you and Guedo?' I interrupted.

Ric paused before saying, 'He work for him. It probably not his choice, none of our choice really,'

'How did he end up working for him though?' I knew I had been right about Mr. Daniels' connection with Guedo. I knew it ran deeper than we had all first assumed.

'Guedo bribed him. he has so many connections. he said if he could get him the job as big boss in NCA then all he had to do was cover a few things up here and there,'

'Just cover a few things up, that's all.' I commented, 'just a few murders, a few rapes, nothing much,'

'So what is Mr. Daniels' actual name?' Neil asked as Ric ignored my reply.

Ric paused before saying, 'we not allowed to tell, no one'a call him by his real name,'

'You can tell *us* though, can't you Ric?' I grinned, he looked at me worryingly-I moved the arm I had the hammer in just to remind him, he shook his head and sighed.

''is name is-er-Marylyn,' everyone sniggered.

'Big man Marylyn, okay then,' Liam chuckled.

'Okay, carry on with the story,' Carlos ordered.

'Guedo just told us to meet him at that place in Brixton the other night, we do what he say-we no-er-nothing'

'So you're just Guedo's skivvy,' I sneered at him.

'No, no. Guedo love us,' he argued.

'Guedo *loves* you?' I repeated, looking up at Carlos' amused expression.

Ric smiled, 'yes, yes, he look scary, he does, but he really a nice, man, nice man,' he stared icily at everyone laughing, 'he still will kill you though.' He warned.

'What's the plan after this, Ric?' I asked him, placing the hammer on the floor.

He exhaled in relief as I done this, so I picked it up again-just to wind him up. A wave of chuckles travelled around the shed, 'the er-plan-er-I dunno. All I know is he transport money to Italy in few weeks,'

'It goes to Italy because he is from there?' Liam asked.

Ric nodded, 'he has home in Italy, Seven lives there now. Mr. D told seven that NCA were closing in, so had to relocate for the time being. Guedo in charge over here now.'

We all shot a look at each other, 'So Guedo isn't Seven?' I questioned, 'Have you met Seven before?'

Ric shook his head. I knew it wouldn't be that easy, if Guedo wasn't seven then who was? They wouldn't be out in plain sight for all to see, it didn't surprise me to hear that he was now hiding out in Italy.

'Unless you want to end up like your friend who shot me, then you're going to help us,' I ordered.

Ric's eyes grew large with worry, 'What friend? What-er-happened?'

'His in the freezer next to the choc ices mate,' I laughed, although the memory of Matt was nothing to laugh about, I enjoyed acting as though I didn't have a care in the world. 'It doesn't matter does it? *You're* still alive, for now.'

'I help though, I-er-been good help,' he argued frantically, 'please don't, I have children,'

I grabbed the bottle of water he had been clinging onto and tipped it slowly on to the floor in front of him, he watched the water as it hit the ground-his eyes filling with tears.

'I know *they* have all been nice to you, but there's no reason for me to be. You tried to kill my friend,' I paused to catch my breath, my leg was still causing me some pain, 'so if you want to see your children again, you better co operate,'

Ric looked me up and down as I crumpled up in pain, 'but they not be nice, they beat me,' he hushed, staring down at his bare feet.

'I think that's nice considering what we could do to you, don't you think?' I warned. 'One more thing. What did your friend Matt-or shall we call him Frosty now?' I paused, 'what did he have to do with all of this?' I still couldn't quite get my head around how Harriet and Matt linked to this organisation.

'Matt...' Ric started to explain.

'Ah, Ah,' I shook my head and raised my eyebrows at him.

'Frosty,' Ric corrected, his worried eyes watching the hammer I was still gripping on to, 'Frosty was like hit man, he just took orders from Guedo to kill, he is someone you not expect, just normal boy. Guedo make him get involved with new girls Mr. D employs so that he can be on the inside too. Think he got a bit too deep with latest one though, talking about love, said he was going to quit and blow the whole thing up in anger once...probably good he dead.'

My heart sank, poor Matt. He was probably so on edge after threatening to talk to the police when I had arrived unannounced at his house. If he'd only let us speak to him instead of pulling out a gun maybe we could have helped each other. Liam was looking at me with an expression that probably matched mine. We wouldn't be telling Billy about this revelation.

'This all very-er-dangerous for you,' Ric cautioned as his eyes jolted around the room. 'I'd give up or you will all die,'

I chucked the empty bottle at him. I could feel Liam's eyes staring at me, I turned to face him and he bit his lip, which was a habit he seemed to have whenever he was turned on. I smiled menacingly at Ric, he seemed to be genuinely frightened of me and that strangely made me feel good.

'Oh don't worry, Ric,' Carlos pretended to reassure him, walking around to the front of him and standing next to me, 'you've been a big help today mate, we won't hurt you. That much,' he ruffled his hair and walked out of room.

Liam helped Jamie up and they followed him. Neil and I stayed for a few seconds longer. I looked down at Ric.

'You, you will be killed,' he warned me.

I towered over him and laughed, 'I think we will be just fine,' but the smug expression on his face angered me even more, I pushed his chair-Ric fell to his side crying, 'don't you dare even look at any of my friends again. Because if you do; *we* will be the ones doing the killing,' I kicked him with my good leg and hobbled out of the shed.

I knocked on the door of Liam's spare bedroom; Jamie's quiet voice invited me in. She was lying on the small, single bed, her hair dripping wet from her shower.

She turned around and smiled at me-sitting up, 'how are you feeling now?' I whispered, placing myself down next to her.

'I'm just really shaken up B. I thought I was going to die,' I didn't know what to say, I still couldn't help but blame myself even after the countless times Liam and Jamie had said it really wasn't anyone's fault. I felt entirely responsible for Jamie being taken. After all, she was my best friend-I had got her involved with it all.

'I'm so sorry,' I murmured.

'B it's not your fault, I told you,'

I grabbed her brush and began running it through her tangled hair, 'it is, I'm just glad you're okay,'

'it's not over though, it's just the beginning,' she sighed.

I knew she was right, there was a long road ahead before we had any type of peace and safety, 'do you want me to sleep in here with you?' I asked her reassuringly as I placed the brush aside.

'No, I just want to be on my own please,' she sniffed as she slid back down onto the plumped up pillow.

'Night J,' I whispered as I turned off her light and creaked the door shut, 'I love you,'

As I brushed my teeth in Liam's dimly lit bathroom, I reflected on everything that had transpired over the past few months and how after being shot, things had started happening very fast.

I felt a wave of adrenaline rush through me again and realized that I was kind of loving this now that we were getting somewhere with our investigation.

I knew that getting so worked up over threatening a man we were holding captive wasn't the best way to get my kicks, but hey, at least I was getting them now. I glanced at my reflection in the cracked mirror above the sink. If I'd doubted it before I would never doubt it again. It's almost as though you could see it in my eyes, I defiantly wasn't the same girl I used to be and the old me was never coming back; that was a fact I was glad of.

I noticed that Liam was leaning against the doorframe observing me as I carried out my bedtime routine, his alluring smile radiated across his exquisite face, a face I knew I would never be tired of looking at.

'What are you smiling at?' I asked through the mirror, as I bent over suggestively to splash my face with the cold running water.

'What do you think?' he whispered, wrapping his muscular arms around my waist and pulling me towards him, his soft lips caressed my neck and, like always, the hairs all over my body stood on end. 'You are amazing Brooke Hamilton,' he whispered, I turned to face him, but before I could say anything he picked me up, my legs wrapped around his waist so naturally as if that was where they had always belonged.

I knew there were a million and one things I should be doing right now, but Liam's holding me was exactly what I needed in that moment. We entered his bedroom and he laid me down so tenderly onto the bed-we didn't even acknowledge the wide open door and the muffled voices of our friends in the living room downstairs.

He stared intensely into my eyes like he always did, and I stared back because I could never look away from him, I wanted to stay in that moment forever, the feeling of passion, tension and danger that had built up over the past few weeks surged between our bodies, our eyes locked together, our hearts were beating perfectly in sync, 'Brooke,' Liam breathed almost silently, 'I love you.'

June
I'm not sure if Liam had just given up, or the fact that a few of us now had nearly died had something to do with it, but over the last month or so he had stopped mentioning his mum as much and eventually the whole situation just seemed to have died down to a halt. It almost felt like a bad dream, I couldn't believe that only a few months ago my life was so crazy.

Mr. Daniels had shocked everyone at work by resigning; we now had a new acting lead on the case until a full time candidate could be found. It was frustrating to still work there knowing what I knew, sometimes I wanted to scream that it was Mr. Daniels all along, but I knew I had to be careful. I wondered if Mr. D had actually resigned, or if Guedo had decided to kill him as well.

Neil and Carlos had released greasy Ric back into the wild, threatening that if he gave away where we'd held him they would be back to visit his wife and children also.

We had tapped his phone and let him know that we would be joining them on their little holiday to Italy. This was probably a stupid move on our part, but we had all agreed that we couldn't take someone else's life, not after the effect that Matt's murder had on all of us.

'More wine?' Auntie Veronica asked as she floated out into her vibrant garden.

'Always,' I grinned, holding up my glass for her to fill. I could see my mother shaking her head in the distance.

Liam was perched on the flower bed next to me, 'so whose birthday party is this again?' he asked for the 100th time.

I laughed and rolled my eyes, 'Sally, our family friend, Auntie Ron loves to a throw a party at your house, don't you?'

She nodded as she took a gulp of her wine, 'oh yes darling I do, especially in the garden with the birds and the bees,'

'Let's not start talking about the birds and the bees,' I joked.

'You have a lovely home, Veronica,' Liam complimented politely. I was very impressed at the effort he was making to get on with my family members. He hadn't yet met my parents, but they were now in such close proximity that I couldn't avoid it for much longer.

'Thank you darling, it's very nice to meet you. We didn't know that Brooke had a secret boyfriend,' she placed herself next to him on the edge of the flower bed.

'I don't think she's even referred to me as her boyfriend yet so don't worry,' he grinned cheekily at me.

'Boyfriend?' My mother's voice bellowed from above me.

'Oh hi mum, Liam this is my mum,' I pointed towards her in a careless fashion, 'mum this is my *boyfriend* Liam,' I smirked at him; this seemed to make him happy.

'So you've been together for a long time?' my mum continued, obviously not even greeting Liam like a normal civilised being would do.

'Yes mum,' I sighed, 'so?'

'Best time of my life,' Liam winked at her. She didn't seem amused. Auntie Veronica cooed from next to him muttering about how sweet he was. I knew that they would get along straight away.

'Just think this is something you should tell your family, don't you Brooke?' my mum moaned. She'd cut her perfectly bleached hair even shorter, which made her look almost pixie like as she always had it tucked behind her ears.

'Not particularly, not if my families opinion of who I associate myself with doesn't really matter to me,' I stated proudly because for once it didn't actually matter if I had their approval. I was happy and so was Liam and that was all I cared about.

Auntie Veronica stood up and walked away, gesturing with her head for Liam to follow-but he stayed put, which impressed me even more.

'So what do you do?' my mum looked down her nose at Liam, who I thought looked extra sexy in his all grey attire.

'I'm a mechanic,' Liam replied, 'do you want to sit down? I can grab you a chair?' he offered. I winced as I knew how hard he was trying.

My mum ignored his kind offer, 'a mechanic, is there much money in that?'

'Mum!' I gasped, but Liam continued smiling, standing up so that he now towered above her eye level.

'I understand that you don't know anything about me, because you and Brooke don't speak that much. But I can assure you that I am defiantly not good enough for your daughter,' he stated.

'You're *not?*' my dad interjected as he had been standing nearby, clearly listening to our every word.

'No, not at all, I have my own house, I work hard, and earn decent money,' he glanced at my mum, 'I have good people around me, I take Brooke out on dates, I make her smile, I worship the ground she walks on. But no, I'm not good enough because no one will ever be good enough for this girl. Not me, defiantly not you and not any future boy she may fall in love with,' I was in shock, I'd never seen anyone be so forthcoming to my mother before, she usually made people cower and shy away.

'You don't think I'm good enough for my own daughter?' my mum raised her eyebrows.

'No, I don't as it happens,' he replied sharply, 'no offence, but if you're not calling her every single day to find out what your amazing daughter has done or how she is then no, you're not good enough. She's incredible and she deserves people around her who make her feel like that, because she is the most perfect person I've ever met in my life.' I smiled and stood up next to him, holding tightly onto his arm.

'Thank you, but you don't need to stick up for me with her,' I smiled reassuringly.

My dad held out his hand for Liam to shake, 'Son, that's all a father wants for his daughter, someone who loves her like that,' Liam shook his hand and thanked him as my mum stormed off. 'Better go make sure the old ball and chain is alright,' my dad joked awkwardly before scurrying off to her side.

Auntie Veronica clapped her hands in glee squealing about how much she loved Liam.

'Was that a bit much?' Liam laughed anxiously, turning to face me and holding my hand.

'I fucking love you,' I giggled placing my hands around his neck and kissing him softly on the lips. 'And don't be silly there are no future boys, just you,'

His smile grew wider and he wrapped his hands around my waist, pulling me in closer, 'oh *really*?' he kissed me again and gazed into my eyes, I forgot that we were at a party full of my family, my knees turned weak and I wondered if he would ever stop having that affect on me. I kissed him passionately over and over again.

'Should probably stop doing that,' he grinned picking me up and spinning me around.

At that moment Liam's phone buzzed from inside his trouser pockets. He pulled it out and examined the screen for a few seconds, before slumping himself back down on the edge of the flower bed.

'What? What's happened? I asked. I hadn't seen this expression on his face for a couple of months now, not since everything had died down. The expression of fear and sadness and pain was painted all over the face that was smiling from ear to ear not 5 seconds ago.

'It's my mum,' he breathed.

'Your mum?' I repeated, 'what, someone's found her?'

Liam passed me the phone, 'no, it's my mum texting me.' I looked down at the screen; sure enough there was a text message from an unsaved number.

The text read:
Liam baby, they've let me contact you because they want this to stop one way or another. Please stop looking into Guedo, I am fine. I am moving to Italy with him. Just get on with your own life and don't worry about me. Love Mum xxxx

'Liam, that could be anyone, I'm sorry, but do you really think that's your mum?' I whispered as a few nosy distant relatives were still eyeing us up after our public display of affection.

'I've left this alone babe, I've kept you safe for months now, I've not mentioned it. But if there's even a 1 percent chance that my mum is alive and texting me I need to know. I'm going to Italy,' he insisted as I passed him back his phone.

'Is that why we stopped looking, to keep me safe? Is that why we just let Ric go, because you wanted it to all go away?' I sat down next to him and watched as he typed out a reply.
'Of course, you were shot and Jamie was kidnapped and Billy, look at how messed up Billy is now. I managed to find the three nicest people on the planet and ruin their lives…' he stopped and glanced at me apologetically.

I looked at him, frustrated, 'hey, you didn't mess *my* life up, I'm so happy I met you! And I'm not one of the three nicest people on the planet; did you see how I behaved when we had Ric? I'm pure evil.' I sighed, it had been nice to enjoy being normal 20 something's, young and in love for the past few months, but I suppose we knew it would always catch up to us in the end. Like Mr. Daniel's had said, we couldn't get that deep in it and not expect anything to happen in return.

'You're not evil,' he managed a smile, 'this is something I have to do though Brooke, please understand?'

I nodded, 'I'm coming with you, and don't even try to argue with me,' I raised my eyebrows as he began to say something, 'I will go with you to the ends of the earth if there's a chance your mum is alive.'

'I love you,' he sighed in defeat, we never argued and this wasn't a time to start now.

August

So there we all were, boarding passes and passports clutched tightly in our hands, waiting eagerly to enter the plane. After Billy had confirmed that the text message had been sent from a town called Portofino in Italy, and that it matched with the location we had found in the emails between Guedo and Mr. Daniels all those months ago, we determined that the likelihood of it being Liam's mum was very thin.

We knew we were most likely walking into a trap from Guedo, or Mr. Daniels, or Seven himself. But we decided to go anyway, because, quite frankly, I believed after everything that had transpired we had all gone totally and utterly mad.

I still couldn't quite comprehend that this was actually going to happen; we were potentially meeting a very dangerous man and we were all standing there with suitcases like we were going to have a lovely holiday. I laughed quietly as I thought how stupid we all were.

There had been a niggling voice in my head since this whole plan had been made that none of us were going to come out of this alive. We were in way over our head, but still we went on, for the sake of Liam. I glanced up at my beautiful, curly haired boyfriend and sighed, like I said, I would have followed him to the ends of the earth if I had to, and it was most likely going to get me killed.

As the queue started to edge forwards, I watched as Billy disappeared into the plane door, followed by Neil and Carlos, eventually it was our turn. We were greeted by an overly cheerful air stewardess wearing the brightest shade of red lipstick I had ever seen on her huge lips, 'oh hello there, let me see your boarding passes, oh perfect, you are in D2,' she rambled on.

'D for doomed,' Jamie remarked from behind me, 'I'm the window seat, you guys sit together,' she insisted as she barged past Liam and I and slumped herself by the window.

As the plane began its journey to Italy, I looked to my right at Jamie already sleeping soundly against the window, then looked to my left as Liam fastened his seatbelt firmly and lent back in his chair.

'We're going to be okay,' I whispered, but I wasn't sure if I was trying to convince him or myself.

After landing in Italy at around 10AM we made our way to the village of Portofino. I watched admiringly as the pastel colours of the houses whizzed by, the fresh air blew through the taxi window, hitting my cheeks as it did so. I wished with all of my being that I was here for different circumstances and that Liam and I had just been a normal couple going on holiday together, but I supposed there could have been worse places to die.

The hotel was beautiful, it overlooked the sparkling blue sea and the stunning pool looked so inviting. We made our way up to the top floor and lugged our suitcases into the large room. Liam looked at me, and then nodded towards the double bed which had been perfectly made with fresh white bedding for our arrival.

'Liam,' I rolled my eyes, 'do you ever stop wanting it?' I blushed, it seemed as though we couldn't go an hour without sneaking off somewhere lately. Maybe it was the impending death that turned us on, but I wasn't complaining.

He shook his head and pulled me onto the bed. 'No, I will never stop wanting you.'

After a couple of hours spent hiding out in our hotel room we decided to take a walk around the village.

We spent the sunny afternoon strolling hand in hand past the high-end boutiques and pastel coloured houses, Liam treated me to ice cream as we perched on the harbour wall and watched in awe as the huge yachts bobbed up and down. Later, we followed a pathway and stumbled upon a museum named *Castello Brown*, there was an art exhibition taking place.

As we wondered aimlessly through the countless pieces of art work I couldn't help but say what I had been keeping in ever since Liam had received that text message. 'Do we have to go tomorrow? Can't we just have a normal life, without all of this trauma and death around us? Isn't this enough?' I span around pointing at all of the amazing scenes surrounding us.

Liam looked at me wistfully, 'Brooke, don't ever think that all of this,' he held my hand and span me around again, 'isn't enough for me, it's more than I ever imagined.'

I sighed, knowing what was going to follow that perfect sentence, 'but it's your mum, I know,'

'Brooke, if you're scared I can do this alone,' he assured me for the thousandth time.

I shook my head in refusal, 'not happening.'

We walked around the village some more, the evening air grew brisk and the sun was starting to set. I grasped Liam's hand in to mine and lent my head adoringly onto his shoulder as we approached a crowd of people gathered around a man playing the piano. We stopped to listen as he finished his rendition of Unforgettable. There were a few soft applauses from the crowd as he shuffled in his chair and prepared for his next song.

'How amazing is it here,' Liam gazed around with the look of a giddy child on Christmas morning painted upon his face.

'Amazing,' I agreed as the beautiful sound of the piano echoed around the cobbled street again. As if Liam's face couldn't light up anymore, he grinned as he heard the notes being played at the start of the song. Of course, just as we walked over a song from *When Harry Met Sally* would be played.

'I think this is the universe's way of saying that we are where we should be,' I smiled at Liam, and in that moment I believed it with all of my beating heart.

'It had to be you, It had to be you,' the ruggedly handsome man playing the piano began to sing as Liam took my hand once more, parading me around in a circle before pulling me towards him and holding me in a perfect ballroom like stance.

I giggled, 'has somebody been taking dance classes?'

'Hey, I know how to move my feet,' he swayed me side to side as he sang along, 'it had to be you, wonderful you, it had to be you,' he was singing so loudly that the crowd seemed to partition in the middle, right where we were dancing.

'Oh abbiamo degil piccioncini qui stanotte,' piano man said through the microphone as he smiled at us. We stared at him with blank, apologetic expressions on our faces.

'Sorry, English,' Liam shouted over to him.

The man carried on playing the tune and laughed at us, 'sorry, sorry, English. I see we have some lovers out here, yeah?' he translated. 'For nobody else gave me a thrill...' he continued the song. I blushed as everyone was staring at us now.

'Better give them a show, Brooke, they're waiting,' he said as he carried on dancing.

'Guess we better,' I laughed lovingly back at him, allowing him to spin me around as he continued to sing so out of tune and so loud. We carried on dancing around the cobbles as everyone clapped and the happy crowd grew larger in size.

My eyes glanced around at my beautiful surroundings as we danced, the sunset, the piano, the song, even the strangers staring at us; and him, oh him. Everything was perfect.

'For nobody else gave me a thrill, with all your faults, I love you still. Baby it had to be you, wonderful you. It had to be youuuuu.' The Piano man and Liam both stopped singing and the crowd erupted with applause and cheer.

'Ay, you got a bigger cheer than me for those moves,' piano man bowed towards us, 'god bless you both.'

I took my place on Liam's chest as we threw ourselves onto the bed in our hotel room and nested tightly into him.

'What a day,' Liam exhaled, 'I'm so happy with you.'

'I love you,' I whispered through the lump in my throat.

'Hey,' he said, tilting my chin upwards so he could look me in the eyes, 'don't be sad about it, everything is going to be fine, we get to be in love and happy like this for the rest of our lives babe,'

'However short that may be,' I added.

'I love you too,' he sighed, obviously too tired for an argument, or maybe deep down he knew I was right.

I opened my eyes a few hours later. We were still lying in the same positions on the bed, fully clothed. I squinted at the bright alarm clock and saw that it was only 1AM. *I still have a good few hours before I die.* I sighed; I glanced up at Liam of whose chest I was still rested on. I knew exactly how I would want to spend my last hours on earth.

'Liam,' I whispered, kissing his neck gently. He squirmed and sat up suddenly, throwing me sideways.

'Sorry, sorry, everything is fine,' I assured him as I wrapped my legs around his waist and ran my fingers through his soft, curly brown hair that I loved so much. 'I love you' I whispered. I looked into Liam's perfect face as he held mine in his hand. 'Whatever happens, I love you.'

He nodded slowly, 'I love you too.' He smiled at me crookedly, before sliding us both to the edge of the bed and reaching for a bag that was hidden in the shelf of the bedside table.

'What's that?' I wondered as I repositioned myself on his lap, not wanting to ever let go.

'Close your eyes,' he ordered serenely.

I did as I was told. I heard the rustling of the bag as he retrieved something from it and the sound of the lamp above the bed being switched on. He took a deep breath in before saying, 'okay, you can open them.'

It took a second for my eyes to adjust to the light; Liam was examining my face closely as he waited for a reaction, I glanced down and there in his hand was a tiny box that had been opened, showcasing the sparkling diamond ring that was sitting inside.

I looked at the ring and then back at his wide-eyed, hopeful face. I pulled myself off of his lap and stood in front of him, shocked to my core. 'You do think we're going to die!' I exhaled, tears pouring from my eyes.

He perched himself up onto his knees and pulled me close to his warm body with one hand, the other still clutching the jewellery box. 'No I'm not going to let that happen, Brooke. Just, just shut up for once and let me do this properly,' he beamed as he clambered off of the bed and placed himself down on one knee, he quickly attempted to sort out his hair and straighten his wrinkled clothes.

My eyes glistened with tears as he started to speak again. 'I've always loved films, especially romance, you know this about me right?'

I nodded, 'of course, most of what you say is quotes from films!'

'Well since the moment I met you I've felt like my life is just one big romantic film, no. it's been *better* than any film I've ever seen'

I giggled at his attempt to remember the speech he'd clearly been rehearsing, 'even better than The Notebook?'

'Brooke, you're even better than the Notebook,' he laughed, 'all these quotes I've collected in my head over the years, all those films I've watched and loved I never *understood* them. And then I met you, oh you…' he grinned up at me, 'I understand what Tom Hanks meant in *Sleepless in Seattle* when he said the first time he touched her it was like coming home, I get why in *A Fault in Our Stars* Augustus said it would be a privilege to have his heart broken by Hazel because my god are you a privilege to love Brooke, and if I die tomorrow then it will be a privilege to die having you love me,' I let out a loud sob, but he continued excitedly. 'You had me at hello, if you're a bird, I'm a bird, to me, you are perfect, here's looking at you kid, all of it, it all makes complete sense to me now.

In *When Harry Met Sally* he says that when you meet the person you want to spend the rest of your life with, you want the rest of your life to start as soon as possible, this is the rest of our life Brooke, being married, being happy, what do you say? Will you marry me?' he breathed for the first time it seemed in that whole minute.

I stared down at him lovingly, his crazy, passionate eyes stared back at me, I wanted to stay in that moment for eternity, 'yes,' I whispered.

'Yes?' he repeated, 'you'll marry me?'

'Yes I'll marry you, my curly haired maniac,' I shouted, 'yes!'

He laughed and jumped up, squeezing me so tightly and lifting me in the air, 'I love you, I love you, I love you,' he panted before sliding the ring onto my finger.

'It's beautiful,' I smiled, tears now pouring down my face.

He cupped my cheeks with his hands and kissed me, 'you're beautiful.'

'Life is not the amount of breaths you take, it's the moments that take your breath away, right?' I smiled. It seemed like an apt thing to say for the situation we were in.

'Ooooh, she's quoting Hitch now people, she's wifey material,' he laughed, spinning me around and kissing me again.

That moment right there, my future husband laughing and loving me so intensely. That was a moment I would never forget. That moment would for sure, always take my breath away.

'We'll tell everyone later,' I whispered as we walked towards the café we'd agreed to meet Liam's 'mum' at, 'let's just get this out of the way first,' I swallowed nervously.

Carlos, Neil and Billy were all waiting for us outside, 'where's Jamie?' I shouted down the pavement at them.

'She's in there,' Billy pointed across the road at what looked to be a little corner shop, 'you know, just in case they blow this place up one of us has to keep the memory of the gang alive,' he joked as we stopped next to him, but I wasn't amused.

Liam and I had stayed up all night celebrating our good news, I didn't want to waist a single second of lying in that bed with him sleeping, I wanted to have him all to myself as much as I could before we pressed the un-pause button and went back to reality that was looming over us.

'Look, before we go inside,' Liam began, but Carlos interrupted him.

'Liam don't even say it, none of us are changing our minds, none of us are scared, if George is in there, we're going in and if she isn't we're still going in because we're not leaving you alone with fucking scum of the earth Guedo okay?' he boomed, he was a man of few words, but when he spoke, people listened.

'Okay,' Liam murmured, 'thank you,'

'Don't get all emotional on us boy,' Carlos said as he ruffled his hair, 'I didn't raise you like that.'

We stepped inside the cosy little café and chose the table in the far corner to sit at. It wasn't busy, there were two other tables filled, one with an elderly man who was tucking into a large breakfast and a strong smelling cup of coffee. And a few seats away from him sat a teenage boy and girl sipping on milkshakes and giggling innocently to each other.

I smiled at how simple their lives looked and hoped that after today mine would be equally as easy. We ordered some drinks and then all we could do was wait.

Liam's leg shook the whole time, Carlos and Neil were as nervous as I'd ever seen them and Billy's eyes shot suspiciously across the room at anyone who made a movement. Me? Well I was full of dread, after the last day here in Italy I wanted whoever was meeting us to just be a no show so Liam would go back to being the happy care-free person he had turned into after the last few months. 'I love you,' he mouthed to me as I glanced over to him.

'Love you too,' I smiled reassuringly back. The bell on the door jingled and a woman wearing a pair of oversized sunglasses confidently strolled in. She was dressed in a clean, nude suit and had her long, dark hair slicked back into a pony tail. I guessed that the expensive looking woman wasn't there to see us and turned back round to face Liam. But to my surprise, all of their jaws had dropped.

'What?' I frowned, spinning back around in my chair to face her again.

She was strutting across the cafe to our table, she even smelt like money. 'Hello boys, long time no see,' she said with conviction. Then, she took off her sunglasses and I knew exactly who she was.

'Mum?' Liam croaked, 'how, how…'

'How, how, how? How am I alive and well?' she mimicked him mockingly as she scraped over a chair and placed herself down next to me at the table.

'Hello, you must be Brooke?' she held out her hand for me to shake, I starred at her hand and back up at her in disbelief.

'You shake it sweetie, let's not get off on the wrong foot now,' she smiled.

I quickly shook her hand, 'sorry, hi. I just, I've always known you to be dead,' I rambled.

She laughed, 'well at least this one can string a sentence together, anyone else?' she looked over at the boys and stared at them for a second. 'Carlos, Neil, you're looking *gorgeous* as ever,' she continued, 'I'm guessing you're Billy?' she tilted her head towards him; 'they said you'd be the runt of the litter. And then there's my Liam baby,' she smiled again.

Liam looked angry, his leg was still shaking and his fist was clenched, the pit in my stomach grew, something didn't feel right at all. 'How the *fuck* are you sitting in front of me right now with your Prada sunglasses looking like *that*,' Liam hissed at her.

'Let me explain...' she leant forwards, 'you probably have a lot of questions,'

Carlos coughed and bellowed above her as she spoke, 'I second that. For someone who is being held captive by her abusive ex boyfriend and a bunch of human traffickers you look pretty good to me,'

Georgina flipped her ponytail jokingly and winked at Carlos, 'why thank you. But I think you have the wrong end of the stick, see all this time you've been looking into these bad people that took me and kept me from seeing my son, did you ever stop to think that maybe I am those bad people?' She raised her perfectly plucked eyebrows. If she'd had a microphone, that would have been her moment to drop it and walk out of the room.

Liam's fist clenched tighter, but he didn't shout. He took a breath and said, 'So you you left me for him…'

'BINGO!' she cried, pulling a gun out from her back and slamming it on the table, 'you, lock the doors now,' she clicked her fingers at the waiter who had served us our drinks.

Panic stricken, he ran to the door, ushering the customers out as he did so. The teenager's milkshakes went flying as they fled and the elderly man jolted up in his chair and followed them as fast as his unsteady legs would allow him to. The waiter slid across the locks and changed the sign to 'closed' before turning back around to face us.

I grabbed onto Liam's hand so tight and didn't let go. 'Go in the kitchen and don't come out, even if you hear gunshots' Georgina instructed him. He sped past us and disappeared into the kitchen.

'Mum, why are there going to be gunshots,' Liam asked slowly.

'I love that you're still calling me mum,' she chuckled nastily, 'even though I'm pointing a gun to you all, you're still holding onto the silly hope that I'm going to pick you up and squeeze you tight and tell you everything's going to be okay because mummy is here now aren't you?' Liam's eyes filled to the brim with tears, I could tell he was holding them back with every ounce of his being, I squeezed his hand tighter. 'Relax, I'm not going to kill anyone today, I don't want blood on my new suit,' she sighed, leaning back in her chair but still gripping onto the gun that was placed on the table. 'As long as you all agree to my terms, then nobody is going to get hurt.'

'What terms?' Neil spoke for the first time since she had walked in.

'You tell me what you know, if you know too much then yes, sadly I am going to have to kill you all. Even you Liam baby. But if you don't, and I'm guessing you don't, then you can walk out of here as long as you never mention it to anyone and you Brooke,' she grabbed my hand, 'you quit your job or you'll end up like Harriet.'

'What did you do to Harriet?' I pulled my hand away from her aggressively.

'Oh she's got fire, I like her for you,' she said to Liam before facing me again. 'See, you don't even know what happened to your pretty little friend. If you must know, Harriet and Matt had decided that they were going to turn us all in. And then *strangely* Matt disappeared,' she raised her eyebrows and patted her nose knowingly. How did she know what had happened to Matt? We had hid that terrible day up so well.

'She couldn't live with herself through the grief and decided that enough was enough, she had to finish what they had started. Silly little girl,' Georgina paused and rolled her eyes. 'So I killed her.' my heart sank. 'More details? Ok... Well Mr. D sent her a text to meet him a day or so after she had told him everything, so of course she jumped at the chance. Then we pulled her into the car and kept her locked up in one of the houses we have going at the moment. Eventually though that annoying girl got rather loud, crying and calling for help so I slit her throat and threw her into the nearest river I could find. Then I moved out here because Marylyn had told me they were closing in on Seven, I couldn't keep getting my hands dirty.'

I cupped my hands over my mouth, feeling as though I could throw up at the thought of poor Harriet and how scared she must have been. I just wished she'd involved me in what she and Matt were planning; maybe we could have helped them.

'Let them out of here, and then I'll tell you everything I know about you, Georgina,' Liam bravely bargained.

'Liam, no,' I argued, 'we're not going anywhere,'

'She's right, they're not,' Georgina cackled, 'I'm not that stupid.' And without a second thought she lifted up the gun, grabbed me and pointed it towards my head.

Liam jumped up in his seat in sheer panic, Carlos and Neil grabbed their guns and pointed them at her.

'Now, now, calm down boys, put the guns on the floor or missy here gets a bullet to her brain,' they reluctantly did as they were told and Liam sat back down slowly.

'Tell me everything you know, and don't leave any details out because we have been watching you and I already know everything you've been doing, this is just…let's call it a little catch up,' she remarked sarcastically.

She pressed the gun harder against my head and dug her nails into my shoulder. I looked at Liam; I wanted him to be the last thing I saw if this unhinged woman decided to blow my brains out.

Billy coughed and edged forwards in his seat, 'I guess we'll just start from the beginning,' his big eyes scanned everyone's faces for approval before he carried on, 'Liam already knew Guedo because he remembered him from when he was younger, all he knew was that he was your boyfriend and he didn't like him-that was it. He knew that Guedo was going to be there the night of the TV interview and wanted to confront him, he thought maybe that you were dead because he'd killed you, I think that's safe to say isn't it Liam?' Liam grunted a graveled 'yes' in reply.

'Okay,' Billy continued, 'It wasn't until he found a few of the things that were saved on your computer that Liam thought that maybe you'd got caught up in something you couldn't handle, but we didn't know what all of it meant. The death of Britney Johnson, we assumed that was aimed at you as she was your friend?'

Georgina cackled again, 'My friend? Oh you really have got the wrong end of the stick. Say Brooke,' she turned me sideways so I could face her, loosening the gun away from my head for a moment, 'if some hoe decided she was going to give Liam her number while you two were dating, would you want that bitch dead?'

'Erm, I wouldn't like her,' I mumbled, shrugging my shoulders.

'You say not liking her, I say wanting a bullet to go through her skull, same difference,' she retorted.

'*You* killed her?' Liam asked, 'what about the note, from Guedo?'

'Guedo left me a note saying this was for me, after he killed her for me, so romantic,' she smiled.

'When did you become so fucked up George?' Carlos questioned sadly.

'We're getting off topic here, continue,' she aimed at Billy as she gripped her hands back around the sleeve of my top, pulling me closer to the gun. Liam looked helplessly at me as I trembled.

Billy went on to tell her everything we knew, in a toned down way. He described the event that happened at Matt's as a misunderstanding and a struggle, saying that we'd only visited the house to check on Harriet because I was worried about her, which was when we came across the pictures of Rebecca and everyone on the wall. He went on to say that once we'd mentioned Rebecca, Neil had felt guilty for not visiting her so that's why we went to see her in prison that one time.

'What about Ric?' Georgina ordered, 'what happened to him?'

The boys shot me a concerned look before answering her, 'Ric's dead, we had to save Jamie that night, I mean you fucking took a 24 year old girl for no reason…' Neil explained.

'…Oh there are lots of reasons why we take 24 year old girls,' Georgina remarked sinisterly. I couldn't believe that an angel like Liam was the son to this absolute monster.

'Ric's dead?' I croaked, 'but we all agreed we wouldn't kill anyone else…'

Billy looked at my guiltily, 'Ric said he was going to hunt us all down and kill us, we didn't have a choice,'

Georgina shrugged, 'the kids right, you didn't have a choice. Ric was an idiot anyway, no loss there.'

'That's all we know, I promise. Please take the gun off of her head now,' Liam pleaded.

Carlos narrowed his eyes at Georgina and sighed, 'she's not letting any of us go Liam.'

Liam shot him a frantic look, 'of-of course she is. We don't know anything, we've proven that now'

Carlos leant over and grabbed Liam's shoulders as he shook uncontrollably, 'there's something we know now that we didn't before though, right? We didn't know your mum was the crazy bitch in charge, we thought it was Guedo. Right, Georgina?' he turned slowly to face her, one hand still clutching Liam.

Georgina laughed hysterically, she really was deranged. 'He's right my darling, I never had any intentions of letting you walk out of here alive. You see, you remember me as mummy dearest who worked so hard to provide a better life for you. But that was never the case. Guedo and I are in love and I would have followed him anywhere,'

'He brainwashed you mum,' Liam couldn't hold back the tears anymore, 'you were a good mum at one point,' he croaked.

Georgina snorted, 'what do you remember? You were a toddler when I met Guedo. He loves me and he wanted me to come with him. I finally had a place in this world. Look at me,' she swung her hair over her shoulder once again, the part of my head where she had been pressing the gun for some time now was pulsating agonizingly. 'I look great, I'm powerful, people listen to me, people are *scared* of me and these silly girls that get themselves taken should take a leaf out of my book before becoming so pathetic and weak.'

'So you're going to kill your own son for a bit of power,' Liam sniffed, 'you're the pathetic one!'

I closed my eyes and attempted to drown out the conversation they were having, it was only prolonging the inevitable, we were all going to die here.

I kept my eyes closed as I processed all of the new information. It was all beginning to make perfect sense now. She was a lost cause long before she went missing; Guedo had made sure of that. Being in an abusive relationship had led Georgina to make some awful decisions. She didn't care about Liam, she only cared about Guedo.

She wasn't on the CCTV footage of the incident with Rebecca because she had helped to set that up, Rebecca had spoken out against Guedo and she had to be sorted out. She wasn't included in the line up on the board in Matt's house because he had never seen her before, she wasn't a victim or a disposable employee like Matt and Mr. Daniels, she was the person in charge, Georgina was Seven.

'G, the seventh letter of the alphabet,' I whispered. 'it's been right under our noses the whole time…'

'Clever girl!' Georgina shrieked, finally pulling the gun away from my head and pushed me forcefully towards Liam. He jumped up and stood in front of me, it was like being in Matt's house all over again.

She stood up and walked over to the front door, unlocking it- for a split second I thought she was going to let us out- but then I saw him walking towards the café, dragging Jamie along with him. I didn't think my heart could sink any lower, but it did.

'Hey baby,' Georgina gushed as Guedo stormed through the door, a few of his minions followed after him dressed head to toe in black.

'My mum is Seven?' Liam sobbed as I grabbed onto his arms.

'Liam, we need to get out of here,' I whispered shakily, 'now!' I watched as Guedo threw Jamie to the floor. 'Jamie! Don't hurt her, please' I begged, but no one was listening.

Guedo clicked his gun and pointing it towards her head. 'This one was hiding across the street,' his gruff voice bellowed throughout the tiny room.

Georgina knelt down to her level and pulled Jamie's chin up to face her, 'hello sweetie, so you're the one that got away?' she studied her face for a moment, 'well you're very beautiful aren't you? There's going to be lots of men who are going to *love* you.' She smiled menacingly.

Jamie looked at me with a powerless expression painted across her pale white face before turning back around slowly and spitting in Georgina's eye. 'Fuck you! Fuck all of you,' she screamed.

Georgina stood up and shrugged, 'shame, we would have made a lot of money with her,' she nodded to Guedo while wiping her eye with the back of her hand.

Before I could let out a cry, the sound of Guedo's gun pierced through the air. Jamie's body fell lifelessly forwards as her blood covered the entirety of the surrounding area.

My knees dropped to the crisp, solid floor with a bang, Liam tried to pull me towards him, but I was frozen on the floor. From that moment on it was as though everything around me was happening in fast forward, whilst I was stuck in slow motion.

I watched through tear-filled eyes as Carlos and Neil grabbed their guns from the floor. Carlos took the first shot, hitting Guedo in the chest. He fell to his knees and grasped the wound while shooting aimlessly around the room attempting to catch Carlos and Neil with one of his bullets.

The gunshots pierced continuously through my ears. Neil had taken care of the 3 other men who were in the room on his own as Carlos strolled over to Georgina and Guedo. Bodies were draped over the tables that not one hour ago people were happily sipping milkshakes from.

Georgina was attempting to pull Guedo out of the café as he grew weaker, but Carlos wasn't going to let that happen. He violently yanked Georgina away with one hand as he pointed the gun at Guedo's head with the other.

Guedo managed to pull himself up slightly onto his elbow, 'you don't want to kill me, you won't find anyone,' he smiled smugly at Carlos.

'Of course I want to kill you.' Carlos shouted back and before Guedo could say anything else a bullet met the middle of his forehead.

Georgina let out a chilling scream, 'NO!' she cried as she frantically tried to pull away from Carlos' tight grip.

Neil ran over to Liam and I, shouting over the cries of Georgina, 'we've got to get her out of here Liam!' I could just about hear him-the ringing of the bullet that had entered Jamie's head was still screeching in my ears.

Somehow Georgina had managed to grab hold of Guedo's gun. Carlos let out a bellowing wail as she shot him in the leg before charging towards us.

'Big mistake!' she screamed. Carlos managed to pull her back which gave Neil just enough time to pick me up and run me out of the building-he threw me to the pavement as he flew back inside towards Georgina and Carlos who were battling it out on the ground. I could see Liam tugging on Billy's arm-who was sat frozen in the seat he'd been perched on since we had entered the café.

'Billy, Liam!' I screamed, 'please come out of there!' Liam looked out the window at me as if he was apologising. I knew what he was about to do. I scrambled to my feet and ran to the door, but he had already reached it. He slammed it shut and locked it. I let out a measly whisper as I banged my fist on the glass repeatedly, 'Liam, please, no!'

'I love you!' he shouted through the smudged window to me, 'I love you so much!' he placed his hand on the glass and I mirrored him as I sobbed. Then his hand disappeared.

'Liam, we're meant to be getting married!' I screamed, 'come out here now!' I watched as he hurdled towards Georgina and grabbed a chunk of her hair, pulling her off of Carlos. I carried on banging the glass frantically, sobbing and screaming, 'I love you, I love you,'

As I watched Liam drag his mum away and pull her into the kitchen area where no one could see him I remembered what he had said the night we met, 'he wants to die a hero, if he had to die, he'd want it to be saving the people he loves most…' I sniffed as I wiped the tears from my eyes and stepped backwards. Carlos and Neil were using all of their strength to pull open the back door that Liam had obviously locked behind him.

 'Billy,' I screamed, 'Billy let me in!' I pleaded, but Billy was still frozen to the chair, staring emptily at the bodies in front of him.

I heard some voices from up above, I stepped backwards again to have a clearer view, somehow Liam and Georgina had made their way to the roof of the building. Some passersby muttered something in Italian at me as I had stepped into their walkway. They were oblivious to what was happening.

The street was quiet and the sun was at its highest point in the sky, making it hard to see onto the rooftop. I could make out Liam holding a gun towards Georgina's head, I sighed in relief. Maybe he would come back to me after all.

I heard the click of the gun and closed my eyes in pure alleviation, but after a second another click followed, and another, each time no gunshot was made. 'Shit!' Liam's voice echoed down to me, my heart raced and I opened my eyes.

Georgina was laughing that hysterical laugh again and I heard her say in a smug voice 'good job I have this.'

There were some shouts of which I couldn't make out, some screams and then a deafening cracking sound rang through the street. I threw myself against the door once again, screaming for Billy to open it or for Carlos and Neil to get through the door and save Liam, but I knew in my heart they would be too late. He was gone.

'Let me in!' I screamed one last time; Billy jumped up in his seat as if he had just awoken from a trance and ran over to me, finally unlocking the door. I pushed him out of the way and ran to Neil and Carlos.

'Something happened! I can't hear them anymore, they were on the roof!' I screeched, throwing myself at the door they were trying to push open still.

'It's useless!' Carlos panted through the pain of his bullet wound.

'There must be another way to get up there,' I shouted as I fled outside and studied the surrounding area. 'There's an alley, maybe that leads round the back,' I called to them, but before they could join me I was gone.

I ran to the back of the building and raced up the metal steps that led to the roof of the café, but there was no one there waiting for me. The roof was empty.

'Liam!' I screamed over and over, but he wasn't there, I knew he wasn't. He wouldn't just leave me like this. I heard a car engine rev loudly, I stood at the edge of the rooftop to see if I could spot the car that was most probably Georgina driving away, and there it was, my heart sank. A pool of blood had been smeared off in the direction of the road beside us, and in it was one of Liam's worn out trainers.

I fell to the floor and let out bloodcurdling scream. My head hit the concrete as I lay drably at the edge of the roof, not caring if I fell off. My best friend and the love of my life were gone; it didn't matter if I died too.

I heard Neil's voice behind me and felt his hand on my shoulder, but I shrugged him away, there was no reason for me to get up off of that floor and keep fighting. They were gone.

365 days later: The beginning and the end

I slumped down on the cream leather sofa, opposite Dr. Daw sat royally in her arm chair.

'Hi, again,' I smiled half-heartedly.

'Brooke, this is the longest you have gone without seeing me, it must have been over a year since our last session?' she asked. She spoke very quietly, but confidently as always. 'What brings you back?'

'It's pretty fucked up,' I stated, 'I wouldn't know where to start,' She chuckled at my brutal honesty, 'well we can only start at the beginning...'

I breathed in, still unsure whether I wanted to delve into the deepest darkest parts of my life, to tell her the whole painful, horrendous truth, but I was sitting in that room again and there was no turning back now, I had to tell someone, and this time I couldn't hold anything back.

'Liam and Jamie are dead,' I whispered. It had been the first times I'd said those words out loud in a year. Dr. Daw's face dropped in shock. She took a moment to compose herself before asking me what had happened. 'We were trying to find Liam's mum...' I began.

'I remember you telling me about this, did you find her?' Dr. Daw interrupted as she placed her notepad and pen on the table next to her.

I nodded, wincing at the memory of Georgina's piercing laugh. 'We found her, and she was linked to the human trafficking organisation I have been investigating at work.' Again, Dr. Daw's face dropped a little more. 'We went to Italy; Liam knew it was his mum that would be there but she-she...' I couldn't say the words again, one time was enough.

'Do you want to tell me what happened?' Dr. Daw asked quietly.

I nodded; I knew that I needed to say it all out loud to make it real, as hard as that was going to be. 'Since leaving Italy a year ago I have relentlessly tried to find out what happened to Liam. I've carried on paying his phone bill just so I can ring and text his mobile everyday in the hope that it isn't real, that one time he is going to answer my call and tell me everything is okay,' I began.

'So you didn't see what happened to him? How do you know his dead?' Dr. Daw asked, attempting to make sense of my scattered explanations.

'He wouldn't leave me like this; there was blood, his shoe…' I closed my eyes as the cracking sound of Liam's body falling from the roof echoed through my brain. It was a sound I knew I would never forget. 'I know there is something wrong, that he can't get to me or, or he is dead. But Even if he is dead, it would be a comfort to have a body to bury, a grave to visit-anything…' I paused and composed myself as my chest grew tighter from the pain. 'Instead it's like he never existed, he has just been taken away from my life as fast as he arrived in it. All I have left of him is his little home, and for the past year I have spent every single night in his movie room watching his favourite films on the old projector, cuddled up in his woolen blanket that he used to wrap me in when I fell asleep. Every night I send him a text with the name of the film I'm watching and his favourite quote from it.'

Dr. Daw smiled sympathetically at me, 'What was last night's one?' she asked.

'Last night was Sleepless in Seattle, 'It was like coming home, only to no home I'd ever known,' I answered. 'I know deep down that Liam isn't seeing these text messages and that me sleeping in my dead fiancé's house spending the nights exactly the same way we used to a year on isn't healthy, but what else am I supposed to do? Accept that he is dead and move on? I don't think that is ever going to happen, Dr. Daw. How could I forget someone who gave me so much to remember?'

'You were engaged?' She asked. I nodded. 'And Jamie, what happened to her?'

'I wake up in a cold sweat every night, dreaming about Jamie's body lying on the floor in front of me. She was shot,' I paused as Dr. Daw winced. 'I don't have my best friend to help me grieve; I don't know what I'm supposed to do without her. It's like I lost a part of myself that day in Italy. I talk to her as if she is still around, whenever I need to vent or cry I pretend that Jamie is there, like she always has been for nearly two decades.'

It had been 6 weeks of inquests before the coroner's office had allowed Jamie's body to be returned home; her parents were distraught and blamed me for her death. My mum agreed with them. According to pretty much everyone I wasn't welcome at her funeral as if Jamie hadn't become involved in my life she would be alive now. I didn't disagree with them; it was a fact I reminded myself of everyday.

Instead, Billy, Dale, Nathan and I had our own funeral for her the morning after her official one. We laid lilies-her favourite flowers- and we spoke of happier times we had all shared with her, I couldn't bring myself to think of anymore darkness, at least not for that day.

After bringing all of the new evidence to light I had received praise and promotions by the dozen at work. We had finally cracked the case we had tirelessly been working on for so long. Mr. Daniels-who was found at an airport attempting to flee the country-had been arrested for the part he played in the organisation and for perverting the cause of justice for all of those years. It turns out that he had decided to resign in an attempt to get away from Georgina and the organisation after they made him kidnap Jamie, but it wasn't that easy. Georgina still had him doing her dirty work by threatening to tip off the police that he had been hiding key evidence.

Thousands of girls had been saved and returned home to their loved ones. I told myself constantly that Liam and Jamie didn't die in vain; if they hadn't of died there wouldn't be evidence tying Georgina and Guedo to any criminal activity.

Georgina had managed to escape Italy somehow and the search for her had been incessant, but she was finally found and bought in for questioning after using her credit card in a small town in Spain. She was later arrested and sentenced to life imprisonment as many of the disgusting men who worked for her agreed to be witnesses in her trial, jumping at the chance to avoid as much jail time as they possibly could.

The trial had answered a lot of troubling questions for me. Rebecca was completely innocent and finally exonerated of all charges after the CCTV footage of Guedo, Georgina and Rebecca entering the pub together was found, along with the text messages between Georgina and Rebecca proving that they were friends and Georgina was the one involved with Guedo, not Rebecca. It seemed that on the last trial Rebecca's defense lawyer was a part of the whole organisation, and that's why significant evidence that could have proved her innocence was never brought forward.

The bulletin board and journals we had found in Harriet's house was her way of linking together enough evidence to bring forwards to Mr. Daniels. From reading through the notes in her journal, it seemed Matt had wanted out of the organisation for some time, but was in so deep that he didn't know how to leave. Harriet had decided to use her resources in the NCA and his knowledge of what went on to build a timeline of all of the events that had and were going to happen. That's why she had skipped so many days at work; she was leading an investigation of her own.

When Harriet had woken up blood stained on the floor and saw that Matt, the boy she was hopelessly in love with, was dead she fled straight to Mr. Daniels for help. Of course neither Harriet nor Matt could have known that Mr. Daniels was involved in it all, he had to keep that knowledge as quiet as possible. Mr. Daniels testified how she was bruised, bloody and hysterical when she showed up to work. He said she spilled everything she knew, and that he recorded it and sent it straight to 'Seven.'

I felt sick at the thought of poor Harriet hopelessly looking for help in all of the wrong places, I wished she had came straight to us-then maybe she too wouldn't be dead.

Billy was fired at work for using their resources without permission, but he said it was worth it. He constantly reminds us of how we should be proud of our achievements as a group of misfits and amateurs. Billy and I stayed as close as ever, along with Dale, Chris and Nathan. It was nice to have some real links to Liam and Jamie still; we spoke about them all of the time.

Carlos got engaged and moved away with his now pregnant fiancé, I guess after all of those years of looking after Liam like a son there was a hole in his life that he needed to fill. He stayed in contact, so did Neil, who had moved to an unknown country with Rebecca. I didn't blame them for running as soon as she was free; I would have done exactly the same thing if I had someone to run with.

I was now head of the NCA department after a thorough inquest had been carried out, I think my job was just about the only thing that kept me going through the darkest times of my life. I had ignored Georgina's threat to quit my job; I didn't care about threats to my life or safety anymore. I had come to the conclusion that if I were to be killed it would be a kindness; it would stop the constant heartache that I felt every waking moment.

'Have you got anyone around you right now?' Dr. Daw broke the silence after a minute or so.

'Auntie Veronica constantly calls me, asking me to move in with her, so does my dad, wanting me to see the twins.' I replied.

'But you don't want this?' Dr. Daw asked as she took a sip of water.

'I don't want to see my parents, or my auntie, or my brother and sister. I don't want to see anyone. I'm not the person they once knew, I wouldn't even know how to act around them anymore. They are better off without me in their lives anyway,' a tear rolled down my cheek as I thought of my family-I shrugged the thought away as quickly as it had entered my mind, there was no way I could start thinking of anything else that made me sad, my heart couldn't break anymore if it tried.

Dr. Daw held up her hand and shook her head before walking over to me and placing herself next to me without making a sound, she often reminded me of Auntie Veronica and how she floated through life.

'Brooke I have known you from a little girl, I have watched you grow through all of the turmoil and upset you have endured, I have watched you come out of the other side as an intelligent, strong young woman and for a while there you seemed like you could be happy...' she spoke.

I looked up at her, 'I was happy, I was so happy,' my voice cracked and the tears continued to flood down my face.

'I know, darling,' she held my hand gently, 'And I know that you didn't come here today for me to say something profound or to practice your anxiety exercises, you came here for a familiar face to talk to, a friend,' I nodded. That is exactly what I needed-a friend.

'We, we were going to get married, we had the rest of our lives ahead of us' I smiled at the memory of Liam's nervous proposal in our hotel room. I wanted to go back to that moment; I wanted to go back there so desperately. I wanted to wrap my arms around his neck, run my fingers through his curly brown hair, look into those beautiful brown eyes and listen to his joyful laugh. I was wrong- my heart could break some more- I felt my chest tighten and the pain soured through it as I realized I was never going to experience any of those things again. I sobbed, I wailed, I screamed until I couldn't breathe, all the while Dr. Daw held onto my trembling shoulders.

380 days after

I had been situated on the uncomfortable bench for some time, the crisp air whirled around me as I clicked my lighter on and off repeatedly in an attempt to warm my hands. The road in front of me had grown busier as time passed; headlights glistened against the evening sky. I glanced down at my phone; the time said **19:26,** my stomach flipped in anticipation. I knew it wasn't long to go, but the minutes seemed like hours and I couldn't wait any longer.

I lowered my gaze back to the rotating doors that I had been watching like a hawk for the past hour, knowing that one of the times they span round the minute would finally be here. Also knowing that I didn't have a clue what the hell I was going to do when that minute came. Would she be angry? Would she have moved on? Maybe she was happier now.

Then, that minute I had been so nervously waiting for finally arrived. The steel doors rotated and there she was. My heart felt as though it skipped a beat, just like before, her pure existence made me melt.

She paused under the shelter of the building and lit up a cigarette, blowing the smoke so elegantly into the air. I watched in awe as the wind gently blew her long, chocolate hair and her pink, silk scarf over her shoulder. I closed my eyes for a second to remember the times she would lay on my chest and I would nestle my face into her hair because she smelt just like coconuts. She strutted to the edge of the road in her thigh high boots, cigarette in one hand and a rolled up newspaper in the other, *oh you haven't changed one bit girl* I smiled to myself.

I knew attempting to explain what was happening wouldn't be easy, and that asking her to mess up her whole life again for me was a selfish move. But I had waited 1 year and 2 weeks for this; 380 days had led me to this very second and I didn't want to spend another moment without her, however crazy things were about to get.

I let out a deep sigh and stood up slowly, waiting for her to notice me as she crossed the road. I stared eagerly as she drew closer and then she realized, and time stood still. Our eyes met and the whole world ceased to exist, the only thing I could see was her. Her perfectly shaped silhouette sparkled majestically against the starry sky; her long hair blew beautifully and her face was still a picture of absolute perfection in my eyes.

To the outside world we appeared to be nothing more than two strangers walking towards each other, but in our world we were so much more than that. We were the reconciliation of secrets and inside jokes, of anguish and pain, of happy days and even happier nights, of unconditional love, of undying passion and lust. All of those things were meeting again for the first time in 380 days and our eyes told the story of how we felt about that.

We were frozen in time for what felt like eternity before Brooke broke the silence with a whisper so quiet that only we, in our world, could hear, 'Liam?'

Printed by Amazon Italia Logistica S.r.l.
Torrazza Piemonte (TO), Italy